MAFIA DEVIL

A M/M Mafia Novella

THE KINGS OF ITALY
BOOK 4.5

MILA FINELLI

MAFIA DEVIL
Copyright © 2024 by Mila Finelli

All rights reserved.

No part of this book may be reproduced in any form or by any electronic or mechanical means, including information storage and retrieval systems, without written permission from the author, except for the use of brief quotations in a book review.

This is a work of fiction. Any names or characters, businesses or places, events or incidents, are fictitious. Any resemblance to actual persons, living or dead, or actual events is purely coincidental.

Cover: Letitia Hasser, RBA Designs

Editing: Peter Senftleben, PSE Editing

A version of this story, originally titled Mafia Brute, appeared in the 2023 Pride Not Prejudice Anthology.

ABOUT MAFIA DEVIL

Amici!

Surprise! I couldn't leave Nikolai and Theo hanging, so here's a short story featuring a Russian mafia boss and an Italian clothing designer. You might remember them as side characters from MAFIA TARGET.

Yes, Giulio and Alessio make an appearance here. Enjoy!

A version of this story, originally titled Mafia Brute, appeared in the 2023 *Pride Not Prejudice* anthology. If you read Mafia Brute, you'll be pleased to see that I've expanded and reworked it here.

Now the languages! MAFIA DEVIL features a mixture of Russian, French, and Italian words. You'll understand why as you read, so I hope it's not too confusing. More fun words to learn and use with your significant other! ;-)

Above all, THANK YOU for reading!

And hey, I'd love an honest review after you're finished, if you feel so inclined.

Remember, join my newsletter for bonus content, book news, and more!

— Mila

"People like to say that the conflict is between good and evil. The real conflict is between truth and lies."

— DON MIGUEL RUIZ

CHAPTER ONE

Nikolai

Paris, France

There is a saying in Russian: *Yesli lyubov' ne bezumna, to eto ne lyubov'*.

"When love is not madness, it is not love."

The madness set upon me, infected me, the instant I laid eyes on him. I could look at nothing else as soon as he walked into the private event.

Tall and lithe, he was dressed in an edgy, androgynous style that reminded me of the glam rock bands of the 1970s. As a boy I'd been fascinated by these bands, men such as David Bowie, T. Rex, and Gary Glitter. When I was twelve I became obsessed with watching videos of Bowie as Ziggy Stardust, and they confirmed what I already suspected: I was gay.

I kept the secret to myself for most of my life. As both a Russian and a pakhan in the Bratva, I would be killed if anyone discovered it. Very few people knew of my sexual preference, and each was loyal to me.

Sipping my vodka, I tracked the man's movements across the room. Tight pants and a blousy, almost-transparent shirt showed off his ropy muscles. Eyeliner and lip gloss. A group of bracelets on each arm. And he wore black leather boots with a heel.

Blyad'! It was like he was crafted just for me, the perfect man for me to fuck.

My dick stirred in my trousers, but this was not the time. I turned away quickly—and found my second-in-command, Ilya, frowning at me. I hadn't even noticed he was there.

Ilya was like a brother to me. We grew up in the Bratva together, our fathers the closest of friends. Now we ran a syndicate in Munich, and I trusted him with my life. Ilya was one of two men under my command who knew my secret.

"What is it?" I snapped when my friend did not speak.

"No."

The one word made no sense. "No, what?"

"To him. No, Kolya," he said, using my boyhood Russian nickname.

"You don't know what I was thinking."

"It was as plain as the ugly nose on your face."

"Fuck off. It was not."

"We are here for business."

He said this as if I was unaware. "Which has concluded."

Because we were based in Germany, much of our product came through France and the Netherlands. One of our banking contacts had invited us to this private party, which was not unusual. Many banks were eager to partner with the Bratva these days, so they tried to impress us with their wealth and influence.

"Even so," Ilya continued, "it is too great a risk."

"I do not require a nanny, *bratan*." Brother.

"If you are considering taking him to the hotel, I would disagree."

I hadn't planned on taking anyone home tonight. It was too risky. But this man . . .

My gaze traveled to where the stranger stood, surrounded by a crowd as he talked animatedly with his hands. The olive complexion made me suspect Mediterranean heritage. Greek? Italian? Was he a celebrity or musician? I had to know. "Find out who he is."

Ilya sighed heavily. "Nikolai."

"Do it."

Ilya knew better to argue. He left my side to get answers, while I remained in the corner, watching and drinking. Was this man gay? I didn't dare assume. All of this might be a waste, if he was straight.

Hope kept me rooted to the spot and my scowl scared away anyone who thought to approach. I was not in the mood for business or small talk. What I wanted to do was watch this man for the next few hours, to soak in every smile and gesture, and commit it to memory. Then I would return to the hotel and use those mental images while I stroked my cock.

"A clothing designer," Ilya murmured when he returned a few moments later. "Theo Barella. Openly gay. Very successful."

My blood thrummed in my veins at the news. Italian. Gay. No ring on his finger and arrived alone.

Perfect.

"You need not stay," I told Ilya, not taking my eyes off Theo Barella. "I will be fine."

"I am not leaving you alone here. I'll wait."

I didn't argue. Ilya took the subject of my safety very seriously. He'd saved my life more times than I could count.

At that moment, Theo moved toward the main bar, a woman at his side. They were laughing together, and my stomach twisted with dark craving. I wanted to shove my dick between those pretty lips, smear the gloss all over his face.

As if I'd said the words aloud, Theo's eyes slid toward me . . . and lingered. He gave me a quick head-to-toe sweep, inspecting me, before returning to my face. I saw the interest there before he looked away—and heat blasted through me.

Fuck, yes.

I left Ilya's side and walked toward the bar. Once there, I edged the man to Theo's left out of the way and leaned against the wood. Then I let my suit jacket brush his arm as I sat my glass on the bar. He flicked a glance at me from under his lashes, but kept up his discussion with the woman next to him.

The bar was crowded, and Theo was not having success in getting the bartender's attention. I withdrew a stack of Euros from my pocket and peeled a crisp one hundred bill from the money clip. With two fingers I lifted it up. A half second later the bartender arrived in front of me. "Yes, sir?"

"Whatever this gentleman would like," I said in French, tilting my head in Theo's direction.

"Wow, that was impressive," Theo said, his French pronunciation threaded with Italian vowels. It was a sexy mix, much like his appearance. "Are you sure, *monsieur?* Because I have very expensive tastes."

"As I said, whatever this gentleman would like," I repeated, my attention still on the bartender.

"Do you have a chilled bottle of Cristal Brut?" Theo asked the bartender, causing me to hide a smile. Did he think seven thousand Euros for a bottle would frighten me?

The bartender looked at me for confirmation and I nodded my head.

"Theo," the woman on his other side said with a giggle. "You are a devil."

A man who brought such joy to those around him? No, he could not come close.

I, on the other hand, was the dark gloom that lurked in corners. The evil everyone feared.

Growing up in Russia, I was called *chort*, or devil, by my mother. She was not wrong. Raised to take over our family's Bratva, I was taught to embrace the violence required to serve as pakhan. And when my uncle died, I ruled without mercy.

But I couldn't remain in Russia, not with a preference for fucking men, so I moved our operations to Germany more than fifteen years ago. It had proven profitable, which was the only reason Moscow hadn't complained. And it afforded me a small amount of privacy for an occasional hookup.

The bartender returned with the bottle, which he promptly opened. He poured a tiny amount into a flute and slid it over to me. I pushed the glass toward Theo.

He picked it up and brought the rim to his mouth. I watched out of the corner of my eye as his lips sealed to the glass and he took a sip. Then his tongue darted out to swipe across his plump, wet lips, and my fingers strangled the tumbler in my hand. I ached to have this man beneath me, screaming my name.

Soon.

"It's big and powerful. Bold," Theo said to the bartender. "I like it."

I paused. Was he talking about me or the champagne?

I waved the bartender away when he tried to hand me a glass. "For the gentleman and his friend." Then I peeled off eight crisp bills and set them on the bar.

"*Merci, monsieur*," the bartender said, scooping up the Euros.

Theo and the woman whispered back and forth before she disappeared into the crowd. Then he edged toward me, champagne glass in hand. "Thank you for the drink. But hasn't anyone told you it isn't safe to carry around so much cash?"

"Do I look like the sort of man a robber would approach?" I knew how I appeared to the outside world. Large and muscled with tattoos peeking out from the collar of my shirt. My ice blue eyes were not friendly or teasing. I was a wolf, a killer walking amongst lambs.

Theo sipped his drink and watched me above the rim. "No, actually. You have a serious don't-fuck-with-me vibe happening."

Time was short, so I decided to cut to the chase. "Do you have plans tonight?"

"Wow." His lips curled into a teasing smile. "You think I am this easy? That one bottle of champagne and I'll go home with you?"

"When I see something I want, there is no point in wasting time."

"I am flattered, but I don't even know your name."

"Nikolai."

Theo stuck out his hand. "Nice to meet you, Nikolai. I'm Theo."

"I know." I shook his hand, enjoying the feel of his warm skin for a beat too long before letting him go.

"Are you Russian?"

"Yes," I answered. There was no hiding it, not with my accent and features. "You are Italian."

"Very good. Most people guess Spanish."

Someone bumped him from behind in their attempt to get to the bar. I took his arm and brought him closer to me. "Would you like to see the view?"

"I don't know. This one is pretty nice." His gaze slowly traveled over my shoulders, then back up to my face. Heat prickled along my skin, the need for him twisting in my gut.

I wanted privacy with him. I wanted to convince him to spend the night with me.

"Come." I took my tumbler and his bottle and walked away from the bar. I knew he would follow. This wasn't only one-sided, not after he eye-fucked me at the bar.

A balcony wrapped the entire length of the restaurant. Ilya nodded once as I headed for the doors, letting me know it was safe, so I went out. Then I headed for the dark corners at the far end of the balcony, away from the light and prying eyes.

Though he didn't speak, I could feel Theo's presence behind me like a electric charge. This craving, this unshakable lust hadn't happened in quite a long time. I wasn't a man driven by my cock. Instead, once or twice a month I used an app for an anonymous fuck and got it out of my system.

This was completely different.

It was foolish to approach a man at a public event. No one except Ilya knew who I was at this party, but still.

"Should I be worried?" Theo asked behind me.

Stopping, I leaned against the rail. "Why would you worry?"

"I don't usually follow strangers out into dark corners. Even handsome ones."

I pitched my voice low, seductive. "I would never let anything bad happen to you."

He sipped his champagne, finishing it, then held the empty glass out to me. "Fill me up?"

My cock twitched, the double meaning cutting through me like a sharp blade. I lifted the bottle to pour more champagne into his flute and noticed that my hand trembled ever so slightly.

Fuck, I needed to pull it together.

I set the bottle on the ground and straightened. "You are a designer."

"Someone has been doing his research," Theo murmured. "Yes, I have my own clothing label, Barella. Maybe you've heard of it?"

"I don't know anything about fashion."

"Your suit says otherwise. Is it Zegna?" He smoothed one hand over the lapel of my suit jacket. I wasn't sure if he was feeling the cloth or my chest. "*Très bien.*"

I took the opportunity to slide my hand onto his hip. "The way you are dressed is very sexy."

"Thank you." He cradled the flute in his hands, not pushing away my touch. "How were you invited to this event, if you aren't in the fashion industry?"

The truth involved laundering payments from large shipments of stolen goods and illicit drugs, so I went with an evasion. "I do business with the company hosting the party."

"The bank?"

"I'm one of their best clients."

While he pondered this, I studied the long sweep of his mascara-coated eyelashes. He was even more captivating up close. Finally, he asked, "Are you a Russian oligarch?"

Better he believed this rather than the truth. "Would it bother you if I said yes?"

"No, not really. In my line of work, I frequently deal with wealthy political types. Never met one from Russia, though."

"I've never met an Italian fashion designer who looks like he belongs in an old music video."

His gaze turned shrewd, calculating. "Which music video? And think carefully—your answer determines whether you get laid tonight or not."

"David Bowie. Or maybe Lou Reed."

His lips parted as his eyebrows climbed his forehead. "David Bowie would've gotten you laid. But Lou Reed? Russian, I might need to marry you."

Before I could say anything in response, he threw back the rest of his drink in one fluid motion. "Let's go to your hotel."

He turned and walked toward the party, and I stayed close behind. I didn't want to let him out of my sight.

Because if I could only have this man for one night, I planned to enjoy every fucking second.

CHAPTER TWO

Theo

The three of us rode up in the elevator.

Yes, *three*.

Apparently, Nikolai never went anywhere without his guards. If he really was a Russian oligarch, it would make sense.

But I found it disconcerting to have this stern, disapproving, obviously armed man in the elevator with us.

What on earth was I doing here?

We were riding to the top floor of the most exclusive hotel in Paris. Nikolai studied his phone, ignoring me, while his guard stood facing the doors, tense and vigilant.

They were both quiet.

It was like a switch flipped the second we exited the car at the hotel. Gone were the teasing glances and flirtatious banter. Now it was all business.

Was this a mistake?

"Do not worry," Nikolai murmured without looking up at me. "A few more floors."

Until what? We check stock prices together?

Or they murder me?

Normally, I used apps for hookups. It was easy and didn't feel as risky as going to a hotel room with a large stranger I met twenty minutes ago.

I unlocked my phone and sent a quick text to my assistant, Sofia.

If I die tonight you can have my leather pants

She sent back an emoji of crossed fingers, that bitch.

"There are cameras," Nikolai said under his breath.

Dai, of course. My shoulders relaxed—until another thought crossed my mind. Did this mean he wasn't out?

I shook my head at my own foolishness. *Oh, Theo. Another closeted man?*

I was like a magnet for them, apparently.

"This had better be worth it," I announced, and I saw the guard's back twitch slightly. Was he laughing?

Nikolai snapped at the other man in angry Russian. I didn't know what he said, but it was hot. Would he teach me dirty words in Russian tonight?

The elevator stopped. The doors slid open, revealing an entry hall, but only the guard exited the car. When I stepped forward, Nikolai held up his hand. "Wait. Ilya will ensure it's safe for us."

When I recovered from my surprise, I asked, "Are there often people hiding in your hotel suite waiting to kill you?"

"Once or twice."

I was joking, but Nikolai was dead serious.

Red flag!

I was five seconds away from requesting a car to take me home.

"You are safe here with me," he added quietly. "Please. Let me spoil you tonight."

The Russian guard reappeared and had a quick exchange with Nikolai. I followed Nikolai into the entry hall, while the guard got into the elevator and left.

We were alone.

"Come." Nikolai strode away, his big shoulders shifting as he moved deeper into the suite.

I pursed my lips, debating as I watched his back. *Cristo Santo . . .* I wanted him to fuck me. If this ended badly, I only had my dick to blame.

Wouldn't be the first time.

Like a fool, I started after him.

The suite? *Mon dieu.* I'd stayed in a lot of hotels in my life, but never in a room like this. A huge open space, it had marble floors with one wall completely made up of glass windows. A baby grand piano sat in a corner, a bar to its right. There were three seating areas, complete with long couches, and two fireplaces.

This was obviously the oligarch suite.

"Would you like a drink?" he asked, slipping off his suit jacket. His bespoke shirt hugged his well-defined chest and shoulders, making my mouth water. Tattoos were visible through the expensive cloth, his upper torso marked with them.

I couldn't wait to trace them with my tongue.

Shaking my head, I walked closer to him. "No."

"Not even champagne?"

I didn't need more alcohol. This was either going to be a disaster, in which case I needed my wits, or this would be un-fucking-believably hot.

In which case I wanted to remember every tiny detail.

So I closed the distance between us, and the way his sharp eyes tracked my approach, with such intensity and heat, caused my heart to race. When we were less than an arm's length apart, I said, "Show me the bedroom."

Instead of leading me farther into the suite, he pounced on me, his mouth capturing mine in a fierce kiss. Heat wrapped around me as he pulled me closer, his big arms holding me in place. His lips were firm, his grip strong. He devoured me with no preamble, just hot, deep kisses right from the start, like he'd been holding himself back and was now free to indulge.

Head spinning, I clutched his arms and tried to keep up.

He licked inside my mouth, and I could taste the alcohol from the vodka he'd been drinking earlier. His tongue flicked and swirled with mine and I breathed him in. Though it was summer, he smelled like winter—crisp and clean with a hint of the outdoors. I struggled for air, but didn't pull back. Instead, I threaded my fingers through his hair and pressed tight to his frame.

A thick ridge dug into my stomach. *Cazzo*, that was impressive. I hoped his dick felt half as nice in my mouth.

While he seemed content to kiss all night, I was impatient. Ripping my lips away from his, I stepped back. His bright blue eyes were dark and hooded, his skin flushed as his chest bellowed. "What are you doing?"

I began removing my shirt. "Taking off my clothes." Nikolai didn't move, his attention riveted on my hands. Gently, I folded the top and placed it over a chair back. It was one of my favorites and I didn't want it torn in haste tonight. "You don't mind, do you?"

"*Nyet*," he murmured absently.

Leaning over, I unzipped my boots and took them off one at a time, each thumping to the floor. When I straightened I flexed my abdominal muscles and unbuttoned my trousers. While I wasn't one for the gym, I was lean and knew how to show off my body to its best advantage. I peeled my tight pants off each leg and draped them over the chair, as well.

Then I was naked.

"No briefs," he noted, his wolfish gaze aimed at my cock.

"The trousers are too tight for them." I stroked myself twice, my bracelets clinking softly. "What do you think? Will I do?"

"Fuck." His fingers flew to his shirt buttons. He was mangling the cloth, poor man.

"Here, let me." I moved in and pushed his hands aside. "This shirt deserves better than torn buttons."

"I want to touch you."

"Go ahead."

Nikolai's big hand wrapped around my shaft and I paused on unfastening his shirt buttons to steady myself. It had been a few weeks since I'd felt the touch of another man, and I'd forgotten how delicious. How *rough*.

He stroked once, my skin sliding through his fingers, and I sucked in a sharp breath. Lust collected in my groin, growing heavy. It was embarrassing how turned on I was, considering we'd just begun.

"You feel good," he said, his deep voice rumbling in his chest and vibrating against my fingers.

Swallowing, I moved a bit quicker on the buttons. I opened his belt and unfastened his suit trousers, then finished with the shirt. He released me to remove his cuff links and shrug out of his shirt.

Madre di dio . . . .

Swirls of ink—various words and icons—decorated almost every inch of his taut skin. He was gorgeous, with very little chest hair to distract from the artwork and muscles. This man had a body begging to be worshipped.

"Theo," he urged, bringing me back to my task.

"*Désolé.*" I returned my attention to his trousers. "You are impressive."

The trousers slid down to his ankles, revealing tight black briefs that were barely able to contain the package underneath. His erection bulged, the heft of his balls cupped by the cloth. Tantalizing me. Challenging me.

I couldn't help myself.

I dropped to my knees.

Looking up at him, I reached for the waistband of his briefs. "I have to warn you, I am very good at this."

"I have been fantasizing about it all night."

He had? I loved sucking cock, so my goal was to best these fantasies. To give him the best blowjob of his life.

I lowered the briefs and allowed his shaft to spring free. *Merda!* It was as impressive as I'd hoped. Long, thick, with a slight curve. Uncut, like me. Large balls, with the wiry hair of his groin neatly trimmed.

Had I died and gone to heaven?

I swiped my tongue along the side, learning the taste and feel of him. When I reached the tip I found a drop of moisture waiting for me, so I lapped it up. "*Délicieux*."

In a blink, he had me on my feet and was carrying me across the room.

Carrying. Me.

A man hadn't carried me before. I hadn't encountered one strong enough, I supposed. But Nikolai held me like I weighed nothing at all, his muscles shifting as he hurried farther into the suite.

I couldn't lie. It was extremely hot.

I nibbled his neck. "If you are trying to impress me, it is working."

"I am not trying, but if this allows me to fuck you tonight then I'm glad."

"You assume that I'm a bottom."

We reached the bedroom and he paused. "No, I never assume. Are you?"

"Yes."

He exhaled heavily. "Thank fuck." In three steps he reached the bed and dropped me on top. I sprawled on the soft duvet, but before I could recover he leaned over and took my cock into his mouth.

"*Cazzo!*" I cried as the hot pressure of his mouth unexpectedly surrounded me.

He sucked enthusiastically and my toes curled. I watched his dark head bob between my legs, his muscled shoulders and arms flexing with his movements. I licked my lips. I could get used to this view.

When he pulled off, I was nearly vibrating off the bed with lust. I would have done almost anything he asked if it meant I could come. "Hurry," I panted. "Condom, lube. *Vite, vite.*"

He took the items out of the side drawer and set them on the bed. "Turn over."

I rolled over eagerly. I was more than ready.

So I was surprised to feel him press my cheeks apart a second before the wet slide of his tongue caressed my hole.

"Nikolai," I gasped and glanced over my shoulder. "It's too much. *Per favore.*"

"I like how you switch between Italian and French. It's very sexy."

"When I'm horny my brain forgets the French. Now, let's fuck before I forget how to speak altogether."

He shook his head. "I don't want to hurt you. Let me prepare you first."

Okay, fair point. He was larger than most men I'd been with, and I hadn't done this in a while. "Hurry, then. Or else I'm going to come."

He took my words to heart, dedicating himself to the task. I clutched the duvet and resisted the urge to hump the mattress as he used the flat of his tongue, then the tip of his tongue, against the sensitive ring of muscle. Then I heard him uncap the lube.

A stream of liquid. The press of his fingers. Pressure, so much pressure. I welcomed it. Shivers raced along my spine and I panted through the burn.

"You are so hot, so tight," he murmured, his lips trailing along my shoulder blade as he pumped his hand gently. "Do you like it?"

"Fuck, yes."

"I am going to make you feel so good, *solnyshko*."

Minchia! Now he was speaking Russian? "Keep going. Say more."

He began a low rumble of words that were both lyrical and rough, and had to be very, very dirty. Combined with his two fingers working inside me, it was overwhelming. "Nic, please. I can't take it. You have to fuck me now."

It only took him seconds to put on the condom and slick himself up. Then he pulled my hips up off the bed and I felt the press of his crown against my hole.

"Breathe," he said, smoothing his hand down my back.

Before I could order him to hurry, he pressed forward, the head of his dick slipping inside. I arched my neck, the ache of his invasion almost too much to take.

Almost.

He waited, perfectly still. Soon, my body adjusted and I could take a breath. I nodded. "Better. Don't stop."

With tiny rocks of his hips he advanced, sank deeper and deeper, until his huge cock was fully seated. He clutched me tight, both of us panting. It was so good, but not enough.

I wanted him to tear me apart.

"Please, *mon grand*." Big man—which was not a lie. To hurry him along, I squeezed my inner muscles, clamping down on him.

"*Blyad'!*"

With that, he began thrusting, pushing, drilling into me. The angle was perfect. He hit my prostate again and again, which caused my dick to leak onto the duvet. I wouldn't last much longer.

Sounds and words were falling from my lips, but I was too far gone to control them. The sensation was gathering in my groin, my toes, a storm that would feel like waves of euphoria. Nikolai pounded my ass, his grunts and gasps mixing with the slap of our hips, and he showed no signs of stopping or slowing down. I was dripping with sweat, delirious, my limbs shaking. So, so close.

I needed to come.

Reaching down, I grabbed my shaft and gave myself a stroke. But suddenly, my arm was ripped away.

"*Nyet*," he growled. "You'll come from my cock or nothing at all."

Whimpering, I hung my head. "You are cruel. I am fucking *dying*."

"You are my little bitch, no? A whore for me to use." He kept thrusting with super-human strength, apparently. "You like the way my cock feels inside you, whore?"

Oh, shit. Fuck.

The unexpected, filthy words tossed me over the edge. My orgasm exploded in every part of me, every bone and cell, even the roots of my hair. I shouted and twitched as my cock emptied onto the duvet, pulse after pulse shooting from the tip.

Nikolai shouted and his thick cock swelled inside me as he emptied into the latex. I wished I could see his face as he came, but I could barely move, my head was so dizzy.

When he finished he collapsed onto my back, and I dropped onto the mattress, right into the wet spot I'd left.

"Holy shit," he wheezed in English.

Then he rolled off me. We were side-by-side, not touching, as we both tried to recover.

Was this the best sex of my life?

I knew without giving it serious thought that the answer was yes.

Nic had stamina, size, a body like a beast, *and* spoke a foreign language?

He might be the perfect man.

His hand caressed my back, tiny brushes of his fingers over my spine. "Stay."

One word, but how could I refuse?

I licked my lips and tried to remember how to form words. "Yes. I'll stay."

CHAPTER THREE

Theo

Three weeks later
On the Mediterranean Ocean

Was I in love?

As I lay on my stomach, slathered in sunblock and moisturizer, sketching designs in the sun, I wondered over these new feelings. How much of this immense happiness came from the warm Mediterranean waters and the glorious food? And this *molto magnifico* yacht?

And how much have I been dazzled by the sexiest man alive?

It made no sense. Nikolai and I have known one another only for a few weeks, not to mention that I swore off relationships ages ago. When you've been lied to again and again, you learn to keep things casual.

If I were a clothing label, it would read: *High heat. Remove promptly.*

Even if I were willing to take a risk, it was very clear Nikolai was not out as a gay man. It didn't take a genius to put the pieces together, starting with his cool behavior in the public hotel elevator. After that, we never once left his hotel room in Paris, and only a few crew members and Ilya were staying on the yacht with us.

So I knew better than to let this go to my head. I've been someone's dirty little secret once and I'll never do it again. Ever.

But for now? How could I complain about such a fabulous holiday?

I adjusted my tiny white swimsuit, one of my own designs. I looked amazing in it, the fabric clinging to all the right places, the color highlighting my Neapolitan complexion. Nikolai couldn't keep his hands to himself whenever I wore it.

I checked my phone and found texts waiting from him.

Can't stop thinking about you

Want to fuck you again

I smiled. As a businessman, I understood the importance of supply and demand. And as a designer, I knew aesthetics, appearance, how to make people desire something they really didn't need. I shamelessly employed all of these skills to keep Nikolai desperate.

I pulled the bottoms of my suit up to give a peek of each ass cheek. Then I took a selfie, making sure he saw plenty of skin, and sent it to him.

Now all I had to do was wait.

To kill time, I resumed my sketching. In two weeks I would be swamped with planning meetings for next year's collection. I had a few ideas, but nothing concrete. I needed inspiration soon. People were depending on me.

Designing luxury fashion was akin to predicting the future. What would people want to wear? Drapes, pleats? What color would be "in?" What trend could I bring back, but with my own special twist?

Nothing came to mind.

And my last collection had bombed. Shapeless, disconnected, and tired were all words that had been used to describe my take on the street wear of the '80s. *Has Theo Barella lost his cool factor?*" one blogger asked. Sales were down and I had been accused of being *boring*. Me, boring!

Now I was full of fear and self-doubt. So instead of working, I doodled one of the Nic's tattoos, a Russian orthodox cross that decorated his shoulder. Except I added flourishes to make it more baroque.

"You are in trouble," a deep growl called out.

Nikolai.

Every part of my skin sizzled as I watched this big, rough man appear on deck. His cream Zegna linen shirt and Brioni trousers fit him perfectly. The man had a closet full of designer clothing, all labels *except* for mine. I tried not to hold it against him.

He looked angry, which made him even hotter. The sun glinted off those frosty eyes and the silver strands at his temples. My lungs suddenly wouldn't pull in enough air.

Now this was inspiration, though not for a clothing collection.

Trying to appear coy, I returned to my sketch, moving my pencil over the paper. "Did you need something, *mon grand?*"

"Hmm." He kissed my shoulder. "I like that drawing. You are very talented." Another kiss. "Creative." *Kiss.* "Sexy."

I grinned, then bit my lip. "Don't stop. What else do you like about me?"

He slapped my ass once, hard. "I will tell you what I don't like. You ignored my texts, then sent me photos to tempt me."

"It was only one photo."

"You know how much I love your ass."

I decided to give him a show. Putting down my pencil and pad, I slowly rolled onto my back and stretched out. Allowed him to see everything God gave me.

His gaze swept my body, lingering on my crotch, and I shivered in response. He had the power to turn me inside out with one glance. "You look good enough to eat," he murmured darkly, his accent thicker. "The most beautiful man I have ever seen. Get inside."

"We should have lunch first." I propped my sunglasses on my head and licked my lips to give them a shine.

"No." Leaning down, he put a hand on either side of my head. His chiseled features were all I could see as he said, "I only want to eat that sexy ass—right before I fuck it again."

While I was in favor of this idea, I decided to tease him. "Don't you have important meetings? I wouldn't want to distract you."

"I am always distracted by you, *solnyshko*. Even when we are apart." Then his eyes softened. Dipping his head, he nuzzled my throat, his lips brushing over the sensitive skin almost reverently. Like he wanted to savor me. "Take pity on me. I am driving Ilya insane. He says I am weak for you."

The giddy, bubbly feeling compounded inside my veins, expanding to warm every part of me. I didn't know exactly what Ilya did, but I knew he was Nikolai's associate. I reached up to stroke Nikolai's jaw. "I like you weak."

"No, you don't." His mouth slid into a knowing smile as he straightened. "You like me strong. Like a bull."

This was true. Nikolai was an absolute beast, and I loved it when he showed off his strength in bed. His endurance and stamina were unmatched.

Grabbing my phone, I unfolded from the lounger and stood. I was average height and on the thin side, while Nikolai was taller and wider than me, bulky from the weights I knew he lifted every morning. I bet all his clothes had to be custom fit. No designer planned for shoulders like these.

I dragged my fingers over his chest. I said in Italian, knowing he wouldn't understand, "*Sono pazzo di te. Ti voglio sempre al mio fianco.*" I'm crazy about you. I want you always by my side.

His fingers latched onto my hips. "What does that mean?"

"It means I'm hungry and you had better feed me first," I lied.

"*Ya khochu prazhit' s toboy vsyu svoyu zhizn',*" he murmured.

"What did you say?"

"That I will feed you later."

Clearly a lie, but I let it go. Glass houses and all that.

My phone suddenly buzzed in my hand.

"Do not answer it," Nikolai groaned, but we both knew work came first. It was something we had in common.

I checked the display. A number I didn't recognize, but it was from France. It could be about work. "I'm sorry," I told him, then accepted the call. "*Oiu, allô?*"

A smooth Italian voice said, "*Ciao*, Theo? I'm sorry to ask, but I need a favor."

It was my friend, Giulio. A former mafia prince, he has been on the run for years, convinced men were trying to kill him. I could hear the panic in every rushed syllable he spoke. I switched to Italian. "Of course, *bello*. Whatever you need."

"Are you still on your boyfriend's yacht right now?" We'd spoken a few days ago, just before Nic and I left Paris.

"*Ma dai*, not a boyfriend. But yes, I am. Why?"

"I need a place to hide out for a few days. Will he mind?"

I glanced up at Nic, who was watching me with a hungry, impatient expression. Risky to assume, but I was confident I could smooth over any of his concerns. I wouldn't turn Giulio away, not when he needed help. "No, he won't mind. How will you find us?"

"I will soon arrive in Nice. I'll contact you then."

"Be safe, *amico*."

"I will." He disconnected.

"Who was that?" Nikolai asked, tilting his chin toward the phone.

Instead of answering directly, I took his hand and began leading him into the salon. This conversation was best had while we were both naked. "Come with me and I'll explain."

When our feet hit the carpet, he pulled me to a stop. A divot formed between his lowered eyebrows, his gaze suspicious. "I'd rather hear it now, Theo."

Did he think I was hiding something?

I closed the gap between us and pressed my front to his chest. Our hips met and I could feel him—thick and perfect and already semi-hard—through the thin fabric of his trousers. Wrapping my arms around his neck, I said near his ear, "A friend of mine is in a tight spot. He needs a safe place for a few days. Do you mind letting him stay on your yacht, *mon grand?*"

Nikolai stiffened, his muscles jerking against me. He tried to step back, but I didn't let him go. "Please," I breathed as I kissed his jaw. "You will like him, I promise."

He didn't soften. "This is dangerous. I do not like guests, especially when I have—"

He bit off what he was about to say. But I knew. The words were as plain as the crooked nose on his face.

Especially when I have a man aboard.

Red flag!

Years ago, when I first moved to Paris, I dated a closeted French politician and our relationship remained a secret for more than a year. At first it was fun to sneak around, but over time I grew to resent how it made me feel, as if I were dirt under his shoe. Unworthy and unloved.

I would not make that mistake again.

Now I lived large and bright, unashamed of my sexuality. I existed in the spotlight, with parties and galas and premieres. I had over two million followers on each of my social media accounts, and my designs were worn by Hollywood celebrities and famous musicians.

I loved every minute of my life.

So this would stay a short fling, nothing more. If Nikolai needed to remain in the closet, fine.

I bit the lobe of Nikolai's ear, scraping my teeth against the sensitive flesh. "He's very private. And gay. Whatever secrets you need to keep, he will not tell a soul."

"I can't risk it."

I couldn't tell him of Giulio's family or of his past. It was too dangerous. So, I grabbed his face in my hands and held him steady as I stared into his eyes. "Do you trust me?"

"Of course."

"Then trust I won't do anything to bring you harm. He is a close friend, and he understands the need for discretion. It's how he lived most of his life."

The lines around his mouth deepened as he frowned. I could tell he didn't wish to deny me, but he was worried about repercussions. "Did you tell him my name?" he finally asked.

"No, and I won't. It will only be a few days. You'll hardly know he's here."

"I don't like it."

No one would be allowed aboard without Nikolai's approval, so I needed to win him over. Hooking a finger in his waistband, I began towing him toward the head just a few feet away. "Let's see if I can change your mind."

CHAPTER FOUR

Nikolai

I was not fooled, I knew precisely what he was doing. But I couldn't stop him. I couldn't help myself when it came to this man.

I should refuse this friend. It's what any sane person in my situation would do. The more people here, the more chance my secret would be discovered.

Blyad'! I needed to say something.

"Theo," I started as we entered the head.

Silent, he shoved me inside and closed the door. With a flick of his wrist, he turned the lock then started toward me. He had an intense, determined look in his eyes. Heat unfurled in my groin, thickening me.

"Relax, *mon grand.*" He moved in, fitting himself perfectly to my larger frame. His hands slid over my chest to the nape of my neck. Drawing closer, he sealed his lips to mine and I sank into his mouth.

I *loved* kissing him. Theo was an active kisser, with his fingers stroking and smoothing, while our legs and chests rubbed together. It felt like we were truly connected, that there wasn't any part of him not touching me.

I lost myself in him, my head swimming with his taste and smell, the feel of warm skin slippery from lotion. I craved more. His touch thawed out my insides, brought back the parts of me long frozen from years of secrets and violence.

More than anything, I wished I could keep this feeling forever. Bottle it up and store it for after this inevitably ended.

I breathed him in, our tongues swirling, and he ground our hard dicks together through our clothes, sending sparks through me. Angling my head, I kissed him aggressively, taking more, demanding all he could give me. I was ravenous for him.

Breaking off from my mouth, he slowly sank to the floor until he was at my feet. But it was his eyes that held my attention. They were filled with hunger and affection, a teasing playfulness that no other lover had dared before. "Take it out for me," he whispered. "Then let me lick you all over."

I was reaching for my belt before he even finished speaking.

My zipper rasped in the quiet room. Then my cock was there, angled at his face.

Theo smoothed his palms up my thighs. "I love that you don't wear briefs on holiday." Before I could comment, he leaned in and put his lips on the crown, kissing the tip. "So gorgeous. Shirt, please."

I whipped off my shirt and tossed it onto the counter. Theo's gaze coasted up my stomach and across my chest. "God, I love looking at you."

"Same, *solnyshko*."

Shuffling closer, he swiped his tongue across my slit. "Yum. Give me more, *mon grand*."

Shit. A rush of lust raced through my balls and I had to briefly close my eyes.

"Yes, that's it." Theo kept licking like I was his favorite treat. He murmured something in Italian, so I answered back in Russian.

"*Mne nravitsya, kogda ty prikasayesh'sya ko mne tam*." I love it when you touch me there.

Theo moaned and sucked the head of my dick into the tight heat of his mouth. His lips were stretched across my shaft, taking me down, more than most were capable of. Fuck, he was good at this.

And he knew what I liked. I was no beginner, but Theo could give classes on how to do this. Men would line up from all over Europe.

"What are you thinking about?" he whispered.

"How good you are at this. You are the best I've ever had."

I wanted to shower him with compliments. Give him sweet words and promises. I was such a fool for this man.

Smirking, he said, "I am fantastic at most things." He bent to nuzzle my balls, sucking one in his mouth as he pumped my cock in his fist. "How fast do you want to finish?"

He knew he could get me there quickly. He was that good. And I had been in the middle of an important call when he sent that selfie. As much as I wanted to spend all day in Theo's mouth, I needed to close the deal I'd been working on. "Be my slut. Eager for my come."

A small smile twisted his lips. He liked this game. He began using his mouth and hand in tandem, swirling and sucking, pumping and squeezing. It was a fucking dream. "So nice," I murmured, petting his hair. "So good for me."

Theo hummed, soaking in the praise. He liked hearing compliments during sex. The more I talked, the more it turned him on.

We were perfectly suited, and it had never been like this with anyone else. When I let myself think about how much I wanted to keep him, it both terrified and saddened me.

I shoved all that aside and watched where he worked me. "That's it," I crooned. "Keep sucking on me. Drain my balls of the come I am storing for you, *solnyshko*."

My shaft was slick with his saliva, the veins visible through the thin skin. His lips pulled while his tongue swirled. Not only that, he used the roof of his mouth, his cheek. The sensation was almost too much.

"Let me see you," I ordered. "Show me how hard this gets you."

He pulled down the front of his tiny suit, releasing his erection. His cock was long and beautiful, just like the rest of him. When he reached to stroke himself, I tightened my fist in his hair. "That is for me, not you. Don't touch it."

He moaned around my dick, the vibration sinking into my skin, and returned his free hand to my thigh. I didn't ease my grip on his hair, instead using the strands to pull him roughly, shoving until I bumped the back of his throat. "You know what I want."

He didn't hesitate. Angling his head, he bent forward at the waist. The resistance around my crown eased and I slid into his throat. I panted, the tight squeeze so fucking good. He shifted closer, taking more, and then he swallowed, the muscles contracting around my shaft. The idea of fucking his throat, combined with the visual of watching him struggle to accommodate me, felt like a gift I didn't deserve.

I caressed his cheek. "So perfect. Take it for me. Let me all the way in."

His eyes darted up to meet mine. They were wide with lust and determination, watery from the blow job. Fuck, he was the most beautiful creature on earth. "Do you need a break?" I asked softly.

He shook his head as best he could, then eased even more of me into his throat. I clenched my jaw, the feeling like nothing else I'd ever experienced. "Fuck, baby. Finish me."

Pulling back, he began tugging and sucking. So as to not to hurt him, I moved my hands to the counter, holding on for dear life as he set his own rhythm. My balls tightened as each stroke and swirl brought me higher, and my insides coiled like a spring.

"Now, *solnyshko.* I am coming *right now.*" The orgasm ripped through me. I began pulsing, ropes of come shooting out of my cock and into his mouth. He moaned again as he drank me down, his throat working as he swallowed. I couldn't look away, even as my eyelids grew heavy. My body trembled with the force of it as the climax went on and on.

When it ended, I slumped against the counter. "Come here."

He rose off the floor and I immediately reached for his dick. My fingers wrapped around him and I stroked the underside just how he liked. Then I held him close and began a stream of soft praise in his ear. "You are so good, so perfect. You like sucking my cock, yes? You're a slut for it. The best I've ever had."

His fingers dug into my shoulders as his eyes closed. "Baby. Oh, shit. God, *Nic,*" he said, the last word almost a whine.

I then switched to Russian, even though I knew he wouldn't understand. But he would hear the tone and know what I was saying. "I feel too much for you, *moya radost'*." My joy. "I wish I could keep you, wake up to you every morning. Keep all your smiles and kisses just for me. For you I wish it could all be different."

A guttural moan tore free from his mouth, and warm jets of come shot onto my stomach. Theo's bottom lip disappeared between his teeth and he grunted, holding onto me as his beautiful face twisted in pleasure. I never tired of watching him orgasm.

I could be shot, bleeding out to death, and still need to see this one more time.

"*Lyubimyj*," I breathed. Sweetheart. I pulled him close, not caring that his come was smearing between us as I kissed him.

When we parted, both of us were breathing like we'd run a race. He rested his forehead against my chin. "*Fuck*. It makes me lose my mind when you speak Russian."

A smile broke out on my face. No doubt I looked like a complete idiot. "You are everything to me," I said in my native tongue.

"Stop." He nipped my jaw with his teeth. "We have things to do, and I'm tempted enough as it is to drag you below."

"Things to do?" I dragged my hand down his back to cup his ass. "What could be more important than fucking?"

He laughed, a light happy sound of pure joy that sank into my bones. "I thought you needed to return to work."

I did. Ilya was probably losing his mind. I was already behind enough in our operations because of Theo's presence on the ship. I couldn't make it worse. I sighed, turned on the warm water, and reached for a cloth on the counter. "Yes, I do."

In seconds the water was warm enough, so I wet a cloth and then began cleaning him off. I took my time, smoothing the soft fabric over his chest and belly, then moved lower. His pubic hair was neatly trimmed, his cock now mostly flaccid and the foreskin back in place. I thought about all the dirty things I'd like to do to him today, and my own dick twitched.

"Even after that blow job, I want you again," I admitted.

Smiling, he kissed my lips briefly, then stepped back to readjust his suit. Once he was covered, I cleaned myself off and pulled up my trousers.

He pushed my hands out of the way and started redressing me. "My friend needs us to meet him in Nice. You'll have your captain point us in that direction, won't you? For me, *mon grand?*"

How could I say no? Even when my gut told me I was making a huge mistake, I nodded.

"Yes, *solnyshko*. For you, I will do this."

CHAPTER FIVE

Nikolai

"This is a fucking mistake," Ilya murmured behind me as we watched the speedboat approach the yacht.

"So you keep saying."

"Yet you do not listen."

"I trust Theo."

"You don't even know this guest's name."

It was true. The man joining us was a friend of Theo's, but that was all I knew. "I am told he is discreet. Gay. Trustworthy."

"Kolya," Ilya said, his voice exasperated. "You are blinded by sex. It is too big a risk."

"Calm down. We will search his bag when he arrives and there is a camera in his stateroom. I will not allow him to learn my true name. It will be fine."

The speedboat grew closer . . . and there were two strangers aboard it.

"The fuck?" Ilya hissed. "You said it was one man."

"That's what I was told."

Theo said it was a friend from Nice. I assumed it was another designer or one of Theo's employees going through a bad breakup. Shit.

Ilya's hands tightened on the rail, the knuckles turning white. "Tell him no. Turn them away."

I wouldn't do that, and we both knew it.

Besides, the boat was upon us. In moments they would be onboard. "Let's go down," I told Ilya.

My friend cursed but followed me as we went below. A fully dressed Theo was in the salon, scrolling on his phone like he hadn't a care in the world.

Before I could say anything, two tall men strode into the room. Both were handsome, with Mediterranean coloring like Theo, but one was clearly a male model or an actor. He was stunning. Was the other man his bodyguard? He carried himself with the bearing of someone with training.

"The bigger one," Ilya said in Russian behind me. "Military."

Yes, I had already come to that conclusion. Theo was on his feet rushing toward the model/actor. "*Bello*! There you are!" They kissed cheeks.

"*Bonjour*, Theo," the man said. "You are looking tan and rested. Paris is treating you well."

"That is what good sex on a yacht will do for you." Theo addressed the other man. "Who is this very tall and handsome man?"

The military man nodded his head in greeting. "Hello. I'm Alessio. Thank you for letting us hide out here."

"So polite," Theo said. "Surprising for an Italian assassin."

Ilya made a choking noise behind me, echoing the horror I felt. I marched over to assess these men for myself. When I put a hand on the small of Theo's back, he linked our arms together. "Giulio and Alessio, this is Nic."

I shook Giulio's hand. "Welcome to my little boat."

"Thank you," Giulio said. "We are incredibly grateful that you have allowed us to stay."

I nodded once, then turned to the military man. Alessio. Instantly,

I noticed something unexpected in his gaze: recognition. *I know who you are*, he seemed to be saying.

Blyad'! It was impossible.

Everyone was staring, waiting, so I held out my hand. "Welcome, Alessio."

We shook, his grip firm like he had something to prove to me. I squeezed harder, tightening my fingers. Did he think to intimidate *me*, a Bratva pakhan?

Ilya touched my elbow lightly and I excused myself from the group. The two of us moved out of earshot so we could talk privately.

"This is a disaster," Ilya said. "The big one brought a rifle on board."

"I saw." I didn't mention that Alessio looked at me with recognition. "Take away the rifle and anything else that might be used as a weapon. Then have security learn everything they can about these two."

We went back over to the group. I slipped my hands into my pockets and tried to appear non-threatening. "We must search your bags and store any weapons in our gun safe. You understand, I'm sure."

Alessio was clearly unhappy at this news. Giulio touched the other man's back intimately and leaned close, whispering something. Ah, so they were lovers.

They handed over their backpacks and the rifle case to Ilya, who took them into another room for a thorough search.

"Now, let me show you to your staterooms. Or, is it one stateroom, *bello?*" Theo began tugging Giulio toward the stairs.

Except Alessio didn't move. He stared at me and crossed his arms over his chest. "I'll be there shortly," he told the others.

Our gazes locked and the mood in the room turned frosty. I heard the concern in Theo's voice as he said, "*Mon grand?*"

My heart pounded, but I strove for calm. I'd faced much tougher adversaries and survived. In thirty seconds I could have both of these Italians killed and tossed overboard.

I called, "It's fine. Get your friend settled and I'll find you on deck later."

Then we were alone. I cocked my head, waiting for him to make a move.

His lip curled. "*Nic.*"

Through sheer force of will, I kept my expression impassive. "Have we met before?"

In fluent Russian, he said, "No, but I know who you are."

How, when I took every precaution to ensure my identity remained a secret?

I switched to my native language, as well. It worked much better for threatening enemies. "I see. And what do you plan to do about it?"

"Does he know?"

A fair question, but I never dragged my lovers into my world. I kept my liaisons brief and then disappeared without a trace. "No. It is too dangerous for him."

"So... you will kill him when you are finished fucking him?"

"Don't be ridiculous." The idea of it soured my stomach.

"There is a reason this secret has never gotten out."

"Because I am careful. I keep my personal life anonymous and discreet." My life in general, actually. Men in my position did not live long, gay or not. I've spent most of my life in hiding, careful never to leave a digital trail.

Alessio didn't appear to believe me. As we assessed one another, I thought of all the ways this could go wrong. Should I put a bullet in his head right now? Theo wouldn't forgive me, and it would cause a whole host of other problems. But maybe safety was more important?

I asked, "Do you plan to tell him?"

"As long as you don't hurt Giulio, then no. I only need a few days here. Giulio is being hunted by Sicilian assassins. Once I learn who they are, we will disappear and you'll never see us again."

His eyes were clear, his expression guileless. It was the only thing keeping him alive at this point. "Good," I said. "Keep your mouth shut and we'll get along just fine."

When he didn't respond, I jerked my head in the direction of the stairs. "You should go and find the others below."

After Alessio departed, I didn't wait. I hurried to my office, where

Ilya was scrolling on his phone. "The assassin knows who I am," I snarled.

"I am not surprised." Ilya paused. "He is Alessandro Ricci."

"The fuck!" I dragged my hands through my hair. Ricci was the best assassin in Europe, a shadowy figure who could eliminate any target, anytime. "He is the one who took out Alexi Zaitsev's brother-in-law in Warsaw."

"This must be how he knows you. You met with Sergei an hour before he was killed."

"A meeting you forced me to do in person against my better judgment. *Fuck!*" I paced a few steps trying to calm down. Was Ricci here to kill me?

I dragged in a deep breath and let it out. "This other man with Ricci . . . Giulio. He's being hunted by Sicilians. We need to know everything about him."

I needed leverage with Ricci and it sounded like Giulio was his weakness. Just as Theo was mine.

"I have security working on it." Ilya put down his phone, his expression grave. "But you have to kill them both. They've seen your face."

"I can't kill them with Theo onboard."

"We are dead if this gets out. Moscow—"

"I know what Moscow will do. And I will take the blame, if it comes to that." I was the one who would be punished. I was the one who slept with men, not Ilya. "And I can't easily kill them."

"You can and you should. They can disappear out here and the sharks will take care of the rest."

A solid plan if not for Theo. I couldn't murder his friends and expect him to keep quiet. So unless I was willing to kill him as well, I was stuck.

But based on my conversation with the assassin, I didn't think murder was necessary at the moment. "The threat of it is enough for now. They know I can kill them. They are at my mercy here, not the other way around. And maybe we can use it to our advantage."

Ilya looked at me skeptically. "How?"

"It would be nice to have the best assassin in Europe in our debt, yes?"

My friend sat back and stroked his jaw. "Could he get in and out of Moscow?"

"They say he can get in and out of anywhere."

"Can he be trusted to keep his word?"

I picked up one of my burner phones. "Let's find out."

CHAPTER SIX

Theo

Nic was acting strangely tonight.

Tension sat in the firm angle of his jaw throughout the meal. I didn't like it. Also, Ilya joined our group for supper. Before this, Nic and I had always dined alone.

I was trying hard to keep the mood light as the five of us ate, but I wasn't a magician. And it was exhausting. There was something going on here that I didn't understand.

One of the crew came in and whispered to Nic, who then rose from the table and buttoned his suit jacket. *Cazzo*, he was handsome. The silver at his temples glinted in the light, and the evening scruff on his face made him look even more dangerous. He came toward me and I wanted to get closer, drag my hands all over him. Crawl inside his skin and stay there. I couldn't get enough.

He draped his heavy palm on my shoulder as he addressed the room. "Please excuse me. I'm sure you all will have fun this evening without me."

I was disappointed he wasn't staying, but I would not beg. "We will certainly try, *mon grand*."

Nic's expression softened and I could see the satisfaction in his gaze as he bent toward my ear. "Do not worry, *luchik*. I will fuck you mercilessly later."

He motioned to Ilya and the two of them quickly left. I lunged for my wine glass. Was the room on fire?

Giulio smirked at me. "I can see you are smitten."

"*Basta!* I'm smitten with his dick, *bello*. You know I don't do relationships."

Giulio pushed away from the table. "Let's go on deck for some air and more wine."

Once outside, I stretched out on a deck chair and toasted them both with my wine glass. "To good friends and good wine."

Giulio put his feet up, then gestured to my kilt-like skirt and distressed black shirt. "Your design?"

"Of course. The skirt is from three seasons ago, but I can't bear to part with it. Do you like it?"

"I do. It's very you."

I'd spent years developing a signature look for my brand, so this pleased me enormously. "Thank you. Wearing it helps to remind me that my creativity isn't completely dead yet."

"What do you mean?"

I traced the rim of my glass with a fingertip. "I owe designs for the next collection in less than three weeks and I have absolutely nothing." It sounded even worse when I said it out loud.

Giulio stretched one arm out on the back of his chair. "You'll think of something. You always do."

"I don't know. I can't stop thinking about the reviews of the last show."

Creases lined Giulio's forehead. "They weren't good?"

"Brutal, *bello*. Brutal."

"Not every collection can be successful," he tried. "You can't dwell on it."

Not dwell on it? How could I forget, when people said I was boring and uninspiring? "I wish it were so easy."

"Have you tried talking to Nic about it?"

"No."

Giulio studied me over the rim of his glass as he took a drink of wine. "Why not?"

"This is not a relationship. I keep telling you. We are fucking, nothing more."

"*Cazzata*," Giulio said. "I saw the way you looked at him tonight."

I swallowed a flippant remark. There was no pretending with Giulio; we'd known each other for too long. I smoothed my already-smooth skirt. "Fine. I think I might like him. It's disgusting."

"You are allowed to be happy. For longer than a few weeks, I mean. What do you know about him?"

I knew Nic kissed me as if his life depended on it, and that he liked to fall asleep wrapped around me. I also knew he often suffered nightmares.

And I knew something was happening between us, something I wasn't sure I could handle.

"Not much. We met at a private event in Paris and I couldn't take my eyes off him. There was an instant spark, like *boom!* He took me outside onto the balcony and we drank champagne under the stars while talking about our love for glam bands."

"Glam bands? From the 1980s, like Bon Jovi?"

"Bello, those are hair bands. *Mon dieu*, did that American school teach you nothing?" I waved my hand. "Anyway, one thing led to another and I swear I've shed five pounds in sweat alone these last few weeks."

"He does look very strong," chuckled Giulio, which caused Alessio to elbow him sharply. "As are you, assassino," my friend murmured to the man at his side.

"It's not just that," I said, unreasonably eager to defend my feelings. "Nic is . . . sweet. Strong, yet tender when I least expect it. When we were in his hotel room, I mentioned I was craving authentic Tuscan *fettunta* and *le bruschette*. The next day he flew in a whole meal from Tuscany for me. All my favorites and more. I nearly cried, the food was that good."

"So what happens at the end of your holiday?"

"Nothing." I looked around to make sure we weren't overhead, then gave voice to my fears. "I'm not sure he is out. We stayed in his hotel room the entire time in Paris. No visitors other than one or two guards. Then he brings me here to this yacht. Either he's closeted or he's embarrassed of me. Or married. Maybe all three."

"Have you asked him?"

"*Ma dai.* Don't be ridiculous. We've known each other for less than a month. I want to enjoy whatever time we have together and not ruin it with heavy conversation."

"You're afraid of the answer."

"*Sì, certo.*"

I've spent enough time around shady men to recognize one. The circles I moved in were filled with politicians and billionaires. Not to mention Giulio, who grew up in the Calabrian mafia. I learned a long time ago it's best not to ask questions.

Giulio refilled our wine glasses. "But are you willing to be someone's secret again? I remember how much it hurt you with that man you were seeing."

"It's totally different, because this is temporary. If Nic keeps me a secret, who cares?"

My friend frowned. "You noticed the crew? The guns?"

Did Giulio think I was stupid? Gorgeous and with amazing style, yes—but not stupid. "Of course. Nikolai is obviously very wealthy. We would be surprised if there weren't guns aboard, no?"

"Perhaps," Giulio said, exchanging a quick glance with Alessio. "But I'm worried about your safety."

This irritated me. Giulio has been on the run ever since his former boyfriend was blown up in a car bomb. Half the time I never knew whether he was dead or alive.

I turned it back around on him. "Fair, then, because I've spent the last four years worried about yours."

"Forgive me. But you know I didn't have a choice."

I wasn't sure this was true, but I let it go. "Where were you before Nice?"

"Scotland. The Upper Hebrides."

I frowned. "That sounds very cold and so very not-gay."

His lips twitched. "It was cold. But I found it surprisingly gay."

"I bet you did. You are pretty enough to make the straightest of straight ones curious." I tipped my head toward Alessio.

When Alessio remained silent, Giulio said, "He's bi."

"Ah." I nodded approvingly. "I can appreciate a man who orders from both sides of the menu."

"What about Nic?"

I paused. "I don't know. We've never talked about whether he's been with women or not."

"You should talk to him more. About your past, about your work."

"There you are," a familiar deep voice said. Nikolai appeared, striding across the deck, and my body began buzzing. I wished I could blame the wine, but it was one hundred percent this man.

I tried to keep my voice light. "*Mon grand!* Come watch the stars with us."

Giulio and Alessio stood to leave, but I hardly noticed. Nikolai settled his bulk in a chair, his eyes never leaving mine. My stomach plunged to my feet. When he looked at me like this, as if no one else existed, he made me feel like the most important, most beautiful man in the world. Like he accepted me, no questions asked.

He patted his large thighs. "Come here, *solnyshko.*"

How could I resist?

I called out an absent goodnight to Giulio and Alessio as they departed, then set my glass down. When I was close enough, Nic latched onto my hips and pulled me onto his lap, then wrapped me in his big arms. I leaned against him, soaking in his warmth. "Would you like some wine?" I asked.

"No. Just you." He kissed my forehead. "Besides, I think you had enough wine for both of us."

"I am not drunk," I protested, but recognized it as a lie as soon as the words left my mouth. "Well, maybe a tiny bit."

He chuckled, not a sound I heard very often out of him. I treasured each one.

His free hand slid under my skirt to stroke my bare legs. "You had fun at dinner. With you friends."

I nodded against his cheek, snuggling closer. "I did."

"It was nice to watch you with them."

"You seemed on edge. Did they make you uncomfortable?"

He didn't answer. Instead, he asked, "What did Giulio mean, that you should talk to me about your work."

"Oh." I ducked my head. "It's nothing."

"It must be something. Tell me."

Maybe it was the wine or the magic of his touch on my skin, but I started telling him of my greatest failure, my latest humiliation. The reviews, the pathetic sales. "And now I have nothing for next year. I'm completely blocked."

"You aren't blocked," he said gently, kissing my temple. "You are mired in fear. There is a saying in Russian, *Volkov boyat'sya – v les ne khodit'*. It means, if you are afraid of wolves, you won't go into the forest."

I wrinkled my nose. "But I am afraid of wolves and I don't want to go into the forest."

He chuckled again, his big chest rumbling against me. "No, *luchik*. It means to forget about your fears and just do it."

"Well, I think Nike said it more succinctly, but thank you." I kissed his jaw. "I appreciate you trying to help."

"You are very talented," he said softly against my hair. "Just look at what you wear, the way you are. You have a gift, Theo. So trust yourself, not the critics."

Warmth suffused me at his praise. "You really think so?"

"I know so. It was what drew me to you in the first place in Paris. No one in that room came close to shining as brightly as you, *solnyshko*."

Heart fluttering madly, I bit my lip and snuggled closer to him. "Careful, or I'll never let you leave this yacht."

"That would not be so terrible."

He continued to stroke my leg, the night sky the perfect backdrop for such a romantic evening. We sat in a long stretch of silence, content to just be together, until he said, "You and Giulio. Did you ever . . . ?"

I couldn't help it. I laughed. "No. He was in love with a close friend of mine who later died. There has never been anything romantic between us." Was this why he'd acted so strangely during dinner? I leaned back to see his face. "Were you jealous, *mon grand?*"

Nic's hand moved higher, past my knee and up to my inner thigh. I shifted to spread my legs ever so slightly. My groin was tightening, my cock responding to his touch as it always did. I dropped a trail of kisses along his jaw.

"Envious of your history," he said. "So yes, a little jealous. I adore you."

It was the closest he'd come to revealing his feelings for me. My chest squeezed. I didn't know what to say.

"Would you—?" He paused and studied my face. "Would you consider another vacation with me? The holidays perhaps, if I can get away."

A burst of pure happiness bubbled up inside me, and I had to close my eyes before I said something stupid. I wanted that so badly. It was only a few months from now. We could sail somewhere warm to fuck and swim and relax together.

But then what? Even if I was willing to break my *no relationships* rule, he was clearly trying to hide me. Hide *us*.

Instead of answering, I avoided the issue by shifting my legs a bit wider. His hand crept higher and he found my surprise.

Nic's eyebrows shot up as his fingertips brushed my balls. "You are bare under here."

I bit his jaw, scraping teeth across his whiskers. "All throughout dinner I couldn't wait for you to find out."

"Fuck," he breathed and wrapped his warm hand around my cock. Then he shifted to kiss me . . . and that feeling of *rightness* settled over me once more. I could drown in this sensation. Nikolai was more potent than any drug or liquor, and each time with him kept getting better.

Our tongues twirled, with his lips pulling and teasing as his fingers worked magic on me. Soon I was fully hard, the skin of my dick pulled tight. The warm night air blanketed us, the sound of the yacht cutting through the water barely audible over our rough exhales. "Do you like your surprise?"

Nic's mouth traveled to lick and kiss the side of my neck. "I like everything about you," he murmured into my skin. "Have you not learned this by now?"

Merda, that was a good answer.

Because I was a masochist, I said, "Tell me what you like best."

He paused his hand and rested his forehead against my cheek. His voice was quiet, but laced with sincerity. "I can't put it into words. You are like a beautiful morning sunrise after years of debilitating darkness."

My heart melted. How could I resist this big, scarred man with his sweet insides? I held onto his jaw and kissed his lips softly. "Let's go below. Then you may tell me what else you like."

His fingers tightened around the base of my shaft, and I sucked in a sharp breath. "What if I want to fuck you here, under the stars, with the whole world surrounding us?"

Then I would let him. I didn't care who saw on this yacht. "Is that what you want?"

He remained silent.

Voyeuristic hopes dashed, I kissed him, telling him without words that I understood. We were already sliding into unfamiliar and dangerous territory, so there was no need to make it worse.

Sliding his hands underneath me, he stood in one smooth motion, holding me close to his chest and carrying me as we continued to kiss. *Cristo santo*, his strength was a huge turn on. He wound his way through the opulent rooms until we reached the owner's stateroom, a gorgeous suite in the bow that overlooked miles of the Mediterranean.

Setting me on my feet, he lifted off my tight black shirt and smoothed his palms over my chest. I quickly unzipped and stepped out of my skirt. Then Nikolai removed his own clothing as I sat to take off my boots. Muscles rolled and popped beneath his tattooed skin, distracting me, and I salivated at the sight of his dick, already hard, when he stripped out of his trousers.

"Get on the bed," he ordered, tilting his head toward the mattress. "Right fucking now."

CHAPTER SEVEN

Theo

I spread out on the bed and fisted my erection, slowly stroking as Nikolai finished removing his clothes and shoes. As I looked at him, various questions about his life—the tattoos, his nightmares—popped up in my head, but I forced them away. I had no right to ask those sorts of things, not when I would be gone from his life in a few days.

He walked to the side of the bed and took out lube and condoms from the drawer. I bit my lip, anticipation surging through me. I wondered what sort of mood he was in tonight. There were times when he was rough and bossy, almost angry, and others when he was tender and careful. Hard to say which I preferred.

Putting a knee on the mattress, he dragged his palm down my chest and stomach, then clasped his hand over mine where I was jacking myself. "You are gorgeous," he whispered. "I want so many things, I cannot decide where to start."

"A kiss would be nice."

The edge of his mouth curled deviously. Instead of giving me a kiss, though, he settled between my legs. "A blow job would be better, yes?"

I stretched my arms over my head, sacrificing myself to whatever my sex god had in mind. "I'm yours, *mon grand*."

A wicked smile broke out on his face before he lowered his head and swiped his tongue across my sac. All the blood in my body rushed south. Then he moved to bathe my shaft with long slow licks, like I was covered in sugar. It was clear he planned to draw this out and I wasn't complaining.

Waves of warmth rolled through me and I closed my eyes, more than happy to let him have his way with me. He swirled the tip of his tongue around the head of my cock. "Keep going." I sank my fingers into his thick hair. "That feels so good."

He sucked me into his hot mouth. My thigh muscles clenched at the rush of pleasure. "Fuck, baby."

He took me deep as his hand kneaded my balls. Then his free hand came up to my chest, where he pinched my nipple. My back bowed in an overload of sensation. "*Minchia!*"

Pulling off with a pop, he looked up at me from under hooded lashes. "Say you'll meet me again. In December." He flicked his tongue across the sensitive head and I shivered.

Warm air coasted over my flesh as he breathed on me, teasing me. "Agree to it, *solnyshko*. Then I will finish you off."

"Maybe you should fuck me instead."

Another lick. "You are being difficult. I know you enjoy what we have together."

I did, but more time with him would only make it impossible to leave later on. "I must return to my life, my career."

Dipping his head, he sucked me again, the tight suction like heaven. My crown bumped against the back of his throat. Fuck, it felt so good.

He kept going, bobbing up and down, faster and faster. I gritted my teeth as I watched my dick disappear into his mouth over and over, and soon the urge to come surged through my groin.

I wasn't ready for this to end.

Panting, I grabbed his hair. "Stop, *mon grand*. I will come if you keep going."

He let me go with a pop. "Get on your stomach."

Eagerly, I rolled over. He grabbed a pillow and slid it under my hips, angling my ass up. "So beautiful," he whispered into the skin of my lower back and began kissing downward. "You will agree to more time, I promise you."

I hid my face in my arms, both pleased and horrified by his persistence over seeing me again. "Where would we go?"

Cazzo, my mouth. Why would I ask such a stupid question?

"Some place warm." He sank his teeth into my ass cheek and my cock jerked underneath me. "Where I can see you in your tiny bathing suit again. New Zealand? South Africa?"

Places where we wouldn't see anyone else. Or anyone we knew.

"I'll take you anywhere you wish to go," he continued as he spread me open.

Then the ability to speak deserted me because Nikolai was pressing his tongue to my hole. I gasped, tingles breaking out all over my body. He hummed and kept at it, his strong hands holding me in place. Sweat broke out on my forehead and I could feel the damp spot where my cock was leaking into the sheets.

And he showed no signs of stopping.

"Are you. Planning to do this. Until I agree?" I could barely speak, my chest heaving as I struggled to breathe.

"Maybe."

Merda. Desperate for friction, my hips started rocking in time with his tongue. Why was I so eager to give this up? A holiday with him in New Zealand sounded amazing right now. "Yes, fine. This December. Holiday."

Straightening, Nikolai wasted no time in getting on the condom and slicking us both up with lube. Then he was there, pushing inside me slowly and giving me time to adjust. He worked steadily, smoothing his hands over my back and hips, petting me. "That's it. Take my dick inside you, *solnyshko*. *Fuck*, you are so hot and tight."

I angled my hips to take more of him—and it was his turn to gasp. He held perfectly still. "Stop. I am trying not to hurt you. I was rough with you last night."

Which I had loved. And I loved that he was taking care of me now.

But I was going to cry if he didn't start fucking me soon. "Please, *mon grand*. I need you. I am dying for it."

With a growl, his hips snapped forward and suddenly he was all the way in. A Russian curse fell from his lips, while I moaned into the mattress. The pleasure was indescribable. Tiny shocks that radiated throughout my limbs, and my vision actually wavered for a brief second.

Then he began thrusting, riding me, and he hit my prostate each time. Waves of warmth rolled through me and, combined with the way my cock was rubbing into the pillow, it wasn't going to be long before I came.

Suddenly, Nic pulled out. I blinked in confusion as I glanced over my shoulder, but he just patted my hip. "Roll over."

"Oh, *missionary*," I teased as I flipped onto my back. "Someone is feeling traditional."

"Someone is feeling like he wants to see your face when you come."

I bit my lip, helpless against this charming side of him. The man had knives and skulls tattooed on his body, but a tender heart. I loved the dichotomy, loved that he didn't fit into a neat box. He was savagely beautiful, like an old Alexander McQueen design. Except with less punk and more Saville Row.

Nikolai lifted my legs and rested them on his massive shoulders. Then he was back inside, giving me that gorgeous dick. My mouth fell open as my lids swept closed, and I resisted the urge to stroke myself.

"You won't let anyone else have this while we're apart," he said, his thrusts too shallow to hit where I needed. "Do you hear me?"

Was he serious? Or was this just sexy caveman talk while we fucked? "*Ma dai*. You expect . . . me to remain celibate . . . until we see one another again?"

"*Da*."

Oh, Russian. So hot. I moaned, the pressure in my groin nearly overwhelming. This teasing was too much. I think I shook my head, but who could tell? "I haven't gone that long without sex . . . since I was twelve."

"You will do this for me."

Yes, I would. God, I would do anything for this man. Never had I felt a connection like this with anyone else before, in or out of bed. It was like we'd known each other for months or years. Decades. An elemental connection that went bone deep.

Speaking of deep, he'd now resumed long strokes that stimulated my prostate each time. My skin turned hypersensitive, like I could feel hairs on the surface. The tips of toes and fingers. My nipples. I arched my back, delirious with need.

"We will both get tested," he continued, like my agreement was a foregone conclusion. "And then I will fuck you raw. My Christmas present will be watching my come dribble out of your hole."

It was too much. On his next thrust I was shooting everywhere, jets of fluid coating my stomach and chest. Some even hit my chin. It was a flood, just wave after wave of blissful pressure. Nikolai kept going, his rhythm never stopping, and my orgasm went on and on until I nearly passed out.

When I sagged into the bed, he let go of my legs. Bending, he ran his tongue through some of the come pooled on my neck. "You are mine, *luchik*."

My heart flipped. I was falling hard, drowning in feelings for this man. It was like he saw into my brain, all the insecurities and flaws, and countered them with his tenacious confidence. He made me feel worshiped and adored, yet valued as a person. Like he wanted to hear my thoughts and learn everything about me. Like I meant more to him than only sex.

It had been ages since that happened.

"Yours," I whispered, unable to stop myself.

Dark satisfaction swirled in his blue gaze, his smile possessive as he looked down at me. Then he was riding me hard, chasing his orgasm. "Watch as I come for you, baby."

As if I could look away.

Never breaking our stare, he let out a roar. His muscles trembled and shook, and I could feel him pulsing inside me through the latex. "*Blyad'!*" he ground out through clenched teeth. The cross tattoo on his neck rippled, as did the star on his shoulder.

He was the most beautiful thing I'd ever seen.

Suddenly, these symbols on his body shifted in my brain—and

inspiration struck. The ideas came to me instantly, so clearly that I could see every piece, every design for next year's collection. Oh, *mamma mia*. Yes, yes, *bello e brutto*.

Beautiful and ugly.

Panting, he slumped over, then slowly withdrew. Sweat rolled down his temples and I wanted to lick this gorgeous beast from head to toe. Affection and happiness mingled in the center of my chest, pulling tight.

I could love him.

Still wearing the condom, he stood and held out his hand. "Up. I am going to wash you in the shower. Then we will watch a movie and discuss our holiday plans before falling asleep."

And I was the world's biggest fool, because I offered up not one single objection.

CHAPTER EIGHT

Nikolai

It was time for another conversation with the assassin.

Yesterday my security man discovered the identity of Theo's friend, Giulio. A mafia prince? No wonder he had Sicilian assassins trying to kill him.

But this made everything more complicated and dangerous for me. I needed answers.

I strode out of my office and went toward the stern. I turned the corner as Alessio went into the head. Giulio and Theo were on deck, laughing and drinking. Good. This would give me a moment alone with the assassin. I sat on the sofa opposite the door and waited.

When Alessio emerged, I said in Russian, "A word."

He didn't appear surprised to see me. Did anything rattle him? Silently, he walked over and lowered himself into the chair opposite me.

"I did some digging," I said.

"Did you?"

"Yes, and I was surprised at what I discovered. Alessandro Ricci." I whistled. "I never would have guessed."

No reaction. "And?"

"And I would like to know what you are doing on my yacht."

He held up his palms, as if placating me. "It has nothing to do with you. I didn't know you were here before I stepped on board."

I wasn't sure whether to believe him or not. "A coincidence. Is that it?"

"I did not choose to come to your yacht."

"And young Ravazzani? Does he know who I am?"

"He knows."

I assumed, but the confirmation pissed me off. "I could kill you, yes? Put a bullet in your head and let the sharks have you."

"And what would your *solnyshko* say about that?"

Motherfucker. I had shown too much last night around Theo. It was clear he was my weakness. My heart was thundering in my chest and I felt cornered—a sensation I hated.

Dangerous, murderous things happened when I felt threatened.

As if he sensed my mood, Alessio spoke into the silence. "My only goal is to keep Giulio safe. I don't care about your secret or your relationship with Theo. As soon as I discover who tried to kill Giulio in Scotland, I will leave to go kill them."

The words seemed sincere. I still didn't trust him.

But I might be willing to let him live. "You will do a favor for me."

His jaw tightened, but he was experienced enough to know how this worked. "You have my word."

"Do you want to know what it is?"

"Why? Are you giving me a choice?"

Smart man. "No, I am not."

"Then we should not discuss it further. I will give you the name and number of my assistant. You schedule it through her." He drew in a deep breath. "And I have a request of my own."

The fucking nerve. I sneered. "You presume to bargain with me?"

"The sooner we discover who wants him dead, the sooner we leave. Do you have an untraceable laptop I can borrow to do some digging?"

I was amenable to this request, as I also wanted the two of them gone as quickly as possible. "I will do you one better. But you must agree to another favor."

I could see the look on his face, the conclusion he'd drawn. I held up my hands. "It's not another job. I don't want—" I flicked a glance at the pair out on deck, then lowered my voice. "I don't want him to know. You and Ravazzani can't tell him. Ever."

"Ever? That is a big favor." He stared at me for a long moment, turning this over. "How do I know what you offer in exchange is worth it?"

"Trust me, it is worth it. How do you think I learned your identity so quickly?"

He pressed his lips together, but said, "Fine."

"*Mon grand!* Were you missing me?"

I turned as Theo approached, the tension in my shoulders easing as I watched him. His body in that tiny bathing suit was something criminal. Sleek lines and smooth muscles, he was every fantasy I'd ever had come to life.

Alessio slipped out of the room, going out on deck, while I stood to greet Theo. I couldn't resist pulling him to me for a kiss, not even caring who saw. "Always, *solnyshko.*"

Theo pushed me into the chair and slid onto my lap. His skin was warm and silky, and I noticed he'd painted his fingernails a deep violet today. I picked up his hand and kissed the back of it.

Theo rested his forehead against my temple. "Do you like my polish?"

"I do. Why purple?"

"First, this is aubergine, and second, because it matches the sweater I am wearing to dinner tonight."

"Is this sweater one of your designs?"

"Yes."

"Then I know I will love it."

He flicked the collar of my shirt. "Why don't you have any of my clothes? Your closet is full of every designer except for me."

Honestly, I had no idea. I never went shopping and hired someone to do it for me. The brand of clothes wasn't important to me—but I was smart enough not to say this to Theo. "I will ask my personal shopper to buy some."

"Don't bother. I will send you some pieces." He smoothed his palms over my chest. "Maybe design a few new ones."

The edges of my mouth curled. "I would like that. I would like to know that you're thinking about me when we are apart."

He sighed heavily. "You know I will be thinking about you. I have a terrible suspicion I'll be doing little else."

My chest expanded with the same strange happiness I only experienced around this man. I'd begged and pleaded for another trip together because I couldn't stand the thought of never seeing him again. The promise of spending the holidays together would be the only way I'd endure the next few months without him.

"Same, *luchik*," I admitted.

Leaning in, he kissed me softly, sweetly. In the way that people who were in love kissed, like they needed the other person's lips to survive. When we broke apart, he whispered, "How are you with phone sex?"

A shot of lust went through my groin at the idea of watching a naked Theo masturbate on my phone. But this was too risky. Impossible for a man like me. When I returned to Germany, where I was based, I would hardly ever be alone. Surrounded by my men, working all hours.

When I hesitated, he tried to pull away. "Forget it. I shouldn't have—"

"I want to," I said quickly, tightening my grip on him. "But my job is demanding and with unusual hours."

How could I make it worse by telling him how dangerous it would be for me if anyone were to find out I was gay? I wanted Theo with me, but I knew it was safer to remain unhappy rather than be together with him.

Disappointment and hurt reflected in his gaze as he tried to shrug it off. "I understand. I'll be too busy anyway."

"Theo—"

Suddenly, Theo straightened on my lap. "*Bello?* Is everything okay?"

Giulio and Alessio were walking toward us, their expressions hard and angry. Giulio tilted his chin toward me. "I need a minute alone with Nic."

Ah, so the assassin had told his boyfriend of our conversation. Was the mafia prince under the delusion there was another option for them? Because I was more than happy to set him straight.

I met Giulio's glare with one of my own. I would not be fucking intimidated, not by anyone.

Theo's voice was filled with worry as he said, "*Mon grand?*"

I appreciated his concern, but I could handle one spoiled Italian boy. I set Theo on his feet, then pressed a kiss to the top of his head. "It's fine, *solnyshko*. Give us a minute."

Instead of arguing, he nodded and walked over to Giulio. They exchanged a few words, with Giulio reassuring Theo that he didn't need to stay and this wouldn't take long. Alessio added a long string of rapid Italian, to which Theo patted his arm before going out on deck alone.

I didn't like the dejected set of his shoulders. He sensed something was wrong, and I had no idea of how to explain it later on.

"My office," I barked and walked out of the salon.

These fucking Italians had caused nothing but trouble for me since they arrived. Ilya was right—I should have killed them right away.

It might be time to rectify that mistake.

CHAPTER NINE

Theo

Something was very wrong.

Clearly, Giulio and Alessio knew something about Nikolai that I didn't. I always suspected Nic had a dark past but, considering Giulio's background, maybe it's worse than I thought.

Sliding onto a deck chair, I let my brain turn this over as I stared out at the water. They just kicked me out of the salon for a private meeting, an assassin, a mafia prince, and a Russian oligarch. What could those three possibly have to discuss?

Red flag!

I'd been sleeping with this man for weeks, had grown close to him. I was *falling* for him. Maybe it was time to admit I wanted more than a fling.

Which meant no more keeping my head in the sand—it was time to find out what the hell was going on.

You knew something was wrong and you chose not to pay attention.

Yes, this was true. All the signs were there. The hiding, the secrecy. The refusal to have phone sex. The guns, the guards. There were so many red flags with this man he was drowning in scarlet.

But wouldn't Giulio tell me if he knew something? My friend wouldn't cover up for Nic—someone he just met. No, Giulio wouldn't do that to me. He knew how I felt about lying. So, what was going on?

I had to find out.

Except when I went back inside, they were gone. Because they hadn't wished for me to overhear?

Another red flag.

I twisted one of the rings on my fingers, wondering what to do. Should I try to find them and demand answers from Nic? Or Giulio? Would they even be straight with me?

Fuck this. I was going to find them. I deserved better than to be shoved aside and lied to. Nic's office. It would be the one place he'd go, knowing I wouldn't follow.

My bare feet made no noise as I crept deeper into the yacht. I wound through the narrow corridors and slowly approached the closed walnut door.

As I raised my hand to knock, I heard voices inside. "...no intention of going into business with Fausto Ravazzani." This was from Nic, and I paused.

Giulio was pitching Nic on mafia business with his father?

My friend spoke next. "That is not what I offered. This would be between you and me."

"And what of Golubev?" Nic asked.

"He's old," Giulio responded, "from another era. You and I could make a lot of fucking money there."

A long silence ensued. Make a lot of money? *Together*? How?

I wasn't a fan of eavesdropping, but nothing could pull me away from this door now. Besides, privacy was for strangers. Not the man you were planning to gift with nude selfies over the next few months.

Nic said, "You have done this before?"

"Of course," Giulio returned confidently. "Frankfort, Hamburg. Zadar, Tirana. Corfu. I haven't stayed in one place very long as a precaution. Once Alessio and I deal with the Sicilians, though, I will be ready to put down roots. Grow my business. Why not Málaga?"

They were talking about Spain, but what business? What had

Giulio become involved in? And why was Nic capable of participating in it? As an investor?

Eavesdropping was supposed to answer my questions, not prompt more.

"I will think about it," Nic was saying. "I will discuss it with my people."

"You do that and let us know," Giulio ordered. "Now, I believe Alessio asked about a laptop to do some digging?"

"Follow me. I'll take you to the security room."

Merda! Were they leaving? I held my breath and wondered what to do. There wasn't anywhere to hide in the corridor—

Giulio's voice stopped me cold. "If I think he is in danger, if I think he should be told, I will do it. He deserves to know the sort of man he is in bed with."

My feet remained rooted to the floor. Me? In danger? From an oligarch?

I held my breath, waiting to hear Nic's response.

Nic growled, "He is in no danger, Ravazzani. Not from me."

"Good," Giulio said. "See that it stays that way."

I frowned at the closed door. My friend—a mafia prince—was threatening the man I was sleeping with . . . not to physically hurt me?

Because this was something Nic was capable of?

I couldn't wrap my head around it.

Then Nic sounded angry. "I am not a fool, nor am I a child. I know the risks and am doing everything to shield him from my life. He will return to Paris next week, none the wiser."

"But perhaps heartbroken," Giulio said.

"But alive," Nic returned.

Alive! *Ma che cazzo?* Because the opposite was a possibility?

Was I so close to death without realizing it?

My blood turned to ice. For fuck's sake, why hadn't anyone told me Nic murdered people in his spare time?

I couldn't take any more. I'd heard enough.

Forcing my feet to move, I darted down the corridor until I found an empty stateroom. Slipping in, I closed the door, slumped against it, and tried to breathe.

"I know the risks and am doing everything to shield him from my life."

Why?

None of this made sense. It was crazy. Was I jumping to conclusions? Perhaps Nic was an important businessman, as he'd led me to believe. He couldn't be a *murderer*. Could he?

I knew dangerous men, including Giulio and Paolo. Alessio. They had certainly all killed people. But I'd never felt unsafe around them.

Though I hadn't slept with any of them, either. I hadn't *loved* any of them. How could I love someone I didn't even know?

I unlocked my phone.

When Nic and I first met, I searched online for information on Nikolai Kuznetsov, only to discover nothing. But I had more to go on now.

I opened up a browser and started typing.

I searched his name, plus this Golubev person they had been discussing. Several Russian websites popped up. I couldn't read any of it, but I scanned them. All the men in the photos had tattoos exactly like the one Nikolai had on a shoulder. A star. Was that symbolic of something?

Another search. This time I got results. The star tattoo meant a high-ranking official in the Bratva.

The. Bratva.

I nearly dropped my phone. *Madre di dio.* The fucking Russian mafia. They were the worst of the worst, with human trafficking and drugs and prostitution.

This was how Nikolai made his money, how he afforded this yacht and the suite in Paris. No wonder why Giulio was worried about Nikolai killing me at the end of our time together. The Bratva were even less accepting of the LGBTQ+ community than the Italian mafia —and that was saying something.

Nikolai couldn't dare risk letting his secret get out.

And I was that secret.

I felt sick. Bending over, I took several deep breaths to keep from throwing up my breakfast. My throat burned with anger and bitterness, mostly at myself. How stupid was I?

Despite all the red flags, I had fallen in love with a monster.

And Giulio *knew*. Why hadn't he told me? I thought we were close. He'd cried on my shoulder for a week when Paolo died. I offered him the use of Nikolai's yacht to stay safe. I would have done anything for him.

And how had he returned my loyalty and kindness? By keeping Nikolai's secret from me. By letting me sleep with a Bratva boss who might very well kill me at the end of our holiday. *Mon dieu*, the betrayal.

The backs of my eyes stung, but there was no time to lose. I couldn't stay here. I had to escape this yacht and everyone on it as quickly as possible.

Straightening, I pulled up my contacts. I found the number for André, a wealthy designer friend.

He picked up on the third ring. "*Bonjour, mon ami!* I thought you were on a yacht in the Mediterranean."

"*Bonjour*, André. I need someone to come get me. Your helicopter, is it available?"

"For you, of course. But tell me. Is everything okay?"

I pressed my lips together, unsure how to answer. We were friends, but I didn't want to drag André into my mess. "There is an emergency at the studio and I need to get back to Paris immediately. The yacht is too slow, *n'est-ce pas?*"

"*Oui, oui,*" André said with a chuckle. "Such are the troubles of your fabulous life, eh? Text me your location and I'll send it for you immediately."

"*Merci.* You are a lifesaver." Perhaps literally, if Giulio's fears over my safety were to be believed.

And fuck him for not telling me himself.

I eased carefully out of the stateroom and went to the helm. This was tricky. I hadn't ventured up here before, so I wasn't surprised by the shocked faces that greeted my presence.

I tried to appear as friendly and non-threatening as possible. "*Excusez-moi.* I am sorry to bother you, but I have an emergency back in Paris. I have asked a friend to send his helicopter to come get me. May I have our exact location?"

The two men at the controls hesitated and exchanged a look. Were they worried I was alerting the authorities to our location, to their Bratva boss?

I went with a lie of my own. "Nikolai is aware that I am leaving." Or he soon would be. "But one of my warehouses caught fire and I am desperate to get back. Can you please tell me where the helicopter can find us?"

"We can't give that information without checking with Mr. Kuznetsov first."

"Of course." I gestured to the phone. "Call him. There isn't a moment to lose."

One of the men reached for the phone and my mouth dried out. Easing closer, I pretended like I was scrolling my phone, not a care in the world, while I was actually zooming in on the control panel and taking photos to send to André.

"He is not picking up," the man with the phone said.

"Try Ilya," the captain suggested.

I waved my hand. "That's not necessary. I'll go find one of them and have them ring you immediately. *Merci!*"

I left, then darted into an empty room to study the photos. Right there, I found it. Longitude and latitude. I forwarded the photos to André. He responded with a thumbs up emoji, followed by a second text:

The pilot said an hour, maybe a little more

I could survive an hour. I could laugh and pretend, never giving the slightest hint of the devastation I felt on the inside. I sent André back a heart.

Then I went to the head and splashed cold water on my face. One hour. That was sixty minutes. Three thousand six hundred seconds.

After that I would go back to Paris, block Nikolai's number, and forget this ever happened.

Cazzo, I was so stupid. All those red flags and I ignored every one.

Recriminations were for later. Right now I needed to keep my cool until I got on the helicopter.

First, I needed to pack. I had to do this quickly and quietly, never giving away that I knew Nikolai's identity. I had no idea what he was capable of. If he wanted to stop me from leaving, he could easily do it, just kill me and dump my body overboard.

I was far too pretty to die.

So my departure needed to be believable. And I needed to give Nikolai a reason not to chase after me. Ever.

On shaky legs, I hurried to my stateroom to find my bags.

CHAPTER TEN

Nikolai

I didn't like lying to Theo.

I wished things could be honest and open between us, but the nature of my life did not allow it. This didn't mean I was immune from feeling guilt over it, though.

He deserved better. I was just selfish enough not to care. I wanted him for as long as I could manage, even if meant not telling him the truth.

For the better part of the next hour, I was distracted by calls, with Ilya listening in. Though I was on holiday, there were many decisions that couldn't wait. Truthfully, being a pakhan was exhausting.

I stared out the window as I listened to Viktor, one of my *avtoritet* in Munich, list his complaints. I barely listened. The weather was beautiful today, and I longed to be on deck with Theo, tasting the sun on his skin, rubbing oil on him. Listening to him chatter on about celebrities and fashion and other things in which I had no interest. Whatever he liked, I wanted to hear his every thought and opinion about it.

I was tired of being alone, giving every bit of my time to the Bratva. Was this all I would have until I died?

Ilya's mobile buzzed. He looked down and then stood, moving away to answer it. I didn't pay much attention. But when Ilya turned and made a slashing motion with his hand, I rubbed my eyes and nodded.

Did it never stop?

Leaning toward my phone, I barked, "Work together or I will cut off your balls, Viktor." Then I disconnected. "What?" I snapped at Ilya.

"Theo went to the bridge and asked about our location. He said there is an emergency in Paris and a helicopter is coming out here to pick him up."

Helicopter?

Emergency?

I shot to my feet. "What the fuck? How long ago?"

"Twenty minutes."

Blyad'! "And they didn't call one of us right away? I'm going to string them up by their fucking toenails."

I hurried to the door, Ilya following behind. He said, "The captain said they tried, but couldn't get through to either of us." When I glared at him over my shoulder, he shrugged. "I told you my service is shit out here."

"Did they give our location to Theo?"

"No, they said they needed approval first. Theo said he would speak to you and then left the bridge."

I would deal with Ilya and the crew later. Right now I had to find Theo. Why hadn't he come to see me? If he needed to return to Paris, then I would find a way to get him back.

Why hadn't he told me first?

Why would he, my conscience whispered, *when you've been keeping so much from him?*

This was different. This was him leaving me.

My stomach twisted into knots. I wasn't ready to lose him yet. I had to find him and convince him to stay. Maybe this emergency could be handled here, or by his assistant in Paris. What could be so catastrophic to pull him away from our holiday?

When I started toward the staterooms, movement on the deck caught my eye. Theo. He was fully dressed and had his bags with him —*all* his bags.

I stopped abruptly and changed direction. "Theo," I called as I approached him.

"Oh, good. You're here." He didn't take off his sunglasses as he gave me a bland smile. His shoulders were tight, his posture rigid. He looked like the time when he found the fast-fashion shirt in my closet and lectured me for thirty minutes about the unsafe labor conditions the company used.

Warning bells began clanging in my head.

"I don't understand. What is happening?"

"I'm sorry," he said. "There is an emergency in Paris. I must cut our holiday short."

"What emergency?"

"A fire in one of the warehouses. I'm sorry, Nikolai, but I really must get back."

"Can't your assistant or someone else handle it?" I stepped in and lowered my voice. "I'm not done with you yet."

His throat worked as he swallowed. "I really am sorry."

Disappointment sank in my gut. "I understand. I'll have the captain turn us toward land. It should only take—"

"There's no need. I called a friend and he's sending out his helicopter for me."

I thought my crew hadn't provided our location? "How did you know where to direct them?"

"I figured out the latitude and longitude. It wasn't all that difficult."

I couldn't see his eyes and I hated it. Why was he being so distant, so perfunctory? This morning I'd had him screaming my name. And now this afternoon, it was like he couldn't get away fast enough.

I cupped his jaw with my palm. "Why didn't you come to me first?"

Instead of melting into me, as he usually did, he held perfectly still. Finally, he propped his sunglasses on his head. His eyes were flat, not sparkling with their normal mischief. "You were busy and there wasn't time. Forgive me."

Ilya was suddenly behind me. In Russian, he murmured, "Helicopter approaching off starboard bow."

Blyad'! Already?

Everything was happening too quickly. My mind reeled with what to do, what to say. I was renowned for staying calm in a crisis, but I felt like I was unraveling at the moment. "I would have taken you to Paris."

"I know. But this is for the best."

"Is that a helicopter?" Giulio and Alessio were walking out on deck, both staring in the distance. "What's going on?"

Theo's voice remained distant as he answered, "I have an emergency in Paris. I'm sorry, but I must leave immediately."

The assassin and Giulio exchanged a look, then the assassin said in Russian, "My rifle. I want it."

"Too fucking bad," I said back. "You won't get it." Ilya and the crew would be armed against a threat, and that was all I needed. I didn't need the assassin armed, too.

The helicopter drew closer. When Theo started to turn, I grabbed his wrist. "Wait."

"Yes?"

When had he turned so cold, so distant? I hated this. I led him into the salon, away from the ears on deck. "I will see you over the holidays, yes?"

"I don't think it's a good idea. We had a nice time together, so let's leave it there."

Blood rushed in my ears and my skin turned hot. A nice time? Had this only been one sided?

I didn't believe it, not after the last few days. I decided to push. "Theo. Please, *luchik*. Let me take you somewhere. A private beach where we can swim and fuck—"

"Are you out?"

The question startled me. My mouth opened, then closed. I didn't want to answer.

I couldn't.

Wind swirled around us as the helicopter landed outside, but Theo and I didn't move. There were so many things I wished to say, but it wasn't possible.

Finally, he stepped back. "Nic, I can't do this. It's clear you are closeted and I refuse to be your secret lover. That's not who I am."

"One more trip. That's all I ask."

"It would be a mistake. We should end this now before someone gets hurt."

Deep down, I understood. But I wasn't ready to say goodbye to him for good. Did he need me to beg? "Please, *luchik,* reconsider. It is not possible for me to be openly gay, but—"

"No." He pressed his lips together tightly and shook his head. "I can't. But thank you for this. I had fun."

Fun? Was that all this had been for him? I reached out, desperate to hold onto him a little longer, but he edged toward the fresh air, toward the helicopter. "I have to go."

Then he was walking away from me. I had no choice but to follow, my chest numb. No one was on deck, though Ilya was no doubt somewhere nearby, keeping watch.

Through the open helicopter door, I could see Theo's bags were already on board. The two of us stood awkwardly by the giant machine. I had an excuse to be confused. But why was Theo so quiet?

"Goodbye, Nikolai." His voice was rushed, like he couldn't wait to be gone.

Not Nic or *mon grand.* Nikolai. So formal.

I hated this. I reached for him and pulled him to my front, needing to wrap my arms around him once more. "Be safe, *luchik.* If you ever need anything, please call me." I'd given him the number to one of my burner phones, and now I would never destroy it.

For a brief second, he sagged into me and pressed his face into my throat. And I swore he breathed me in, like he was trying to memorize my scent. Or maybe this was what I was doing to him, who the fuck knew?

Without another word, he squeezed my shoulder and pulled away. Panic filled me, a fist squeezing my insides. But I could do nothing.

Then he climbed inside. He gave me a small, strained smile before the door shut. The helicopter was soon up in the air, carrying him away from me.

I couldn't move, my feet rooted to the deck. I stood there watching. Gone. He was gone. I couldn't wrap my head around it. I hadn't prepared for this.

When I could no longer see the helicopter, I went into the salon. There I poured a large glass of strong Russian vodka, the kind I drank when I wanted to get drunk.

I had just finished my second glass when Ilya came in with a tablet. "You need to see this," he said.

"Not now. I want to drink until I pass out."

"Trust me. You will want to see it." He lowered himself next to me and unlocked the device. He had the yacht's security software loaded up. "Watch."

Video from one of the cameras began playing. It was Theo. He was in the corridor outside my office, poised at the door, *eavesdropping*. I straightened, my body on alert. "When was this?"

"When we were meeting with Ravazzani and Ricci."

Blyad'! Had Theo overheard our discussion? Nothing specific was mentioned of my position, I don't think, but the context would've made it clear I was a criminal.

"Now watch this one," Ilya said, pushing some buttons. "This one you will definitely want to see."

He pressed the button. It was Theo, texting in one of the empty staterooms. His thumbs flew over the keyboard, then he swiped on the glass. Opening an app? He frowned, lines of frustration creasing his brow as he continued to scroll and type on his phone.

Then he jerked in surprise.

He peered closer at his phone, his eyes round and wide. A second later he slumped against the wall. The look on his face . . . it was ravaged. Destroyed. Surprise and confusion, followed by hurt and fear. And I knew this was the moment.

This was the moment he learned who I was—*what* I was.

Fuck.

My throat closed as I watched the man I loved bend over at the waist, like he might get sick.

I make him sick.

The knot in my chest twisted, strangling me. Theo's body curled in on itself so I could not see his face, but I didn't need to. I could practically sense his pain, his utter devastation. My secrets were too much for him, and now he knew the truth.

"Are you out?"

A much easier question to ask instead of, *Are you in the Bratva?* No wonder he rushed to get away from me.

"Enough," I said, shoving the tablet away. I could not look at this any longer. It was breaking my heart.

"What are you going to do?" Ilya studied me. "This is very bad for us."

"He will not tell anyone."

"You do not know this. He could—"

"He won't!" I snapped. "He is not cruel or vindictive, not like *us.*" Theo would want to forget me, return to his life of loud parties and bright lights, leaving my shadows and darkness behind.

And I loved him enough to let him. He belonged there, in the spotlight for everyone to adore. He was never mine to keep anyway. I couldn't leave the Bratva and Theo could never join it, even if he wanted to.

I propped my elbows on my knees and stared down at my feet. *Fuck.* I hadn't expected this to hurt so badly.

"I am sorry, Kolya," Ilya said softly as he stood up.

Yes, I was also sorry. But after a life spent as a brutal criminal, I knew there was no time for weakness. No time for heartache or wishing my life was any different.

I had an empire to run.

"Kick the Italians off the yacht. Then let's return to Munich," I told Ilya. "We've been away too long."

And maybe while there I could forget.

CHAPTER ELEVEN

Nikolai

Munich, Germany
One month later

I stared at the mess on the ground.

Someone clapped my shoulder, jostling me. "He's dead, Nikolai."

Glancing up, I handed my knife to Ilya. "Clean this trash up," I barked at my men. They nodded quickly, no one quite meeting my eyes.

This one had been especially brutal.

I turned and left the cellar, climbing the stairs that led to my office. There, I could wash the blood off.

"You are getting worse," Ilya dared to mutter behind me.

I said nothing, just continued up the steps.

"How long do you think you can keep going like this?"

I threw open the office door and tried to close it behind me. Ilya pushed through, not caring that I might wish to be alone. I snarled, "Fuck off, Ilya."

"No, my friend. I am staying until you see reason."

"And what reason should I see? That we are more profitable and destroying our enemies at a faster clip, yes? This is what you are complaining about?" I snorted and went to wash my hands.

When I emerged Ilya was still there, waiting for me. I sat behind my desk and ignored him.

"Kolya," he said quietly. "Two weeks ago, I was concerned. Last week? Panicked. Today I am terrified."

"I am no danger to you," I scoffed.

"I am not scared of you. I am scared *for* you." He cocked his head. "In all our years together, I have never seen this. Are you trying to get yourself killed? Is this the only solution to your problem?"

I unlocked my phone and began scrolling through my messages. "I am fine. You need to stop worrying so much."

"You are reckless," he snapped. "And you will start a war if you are not careful."

My only thought was, *Who cares?*

What difference did it make? Theo was gone, back in Paris. Last week I broke down and searched for him online. I found photos of him at a recent event, looking tired but happy. The images were like an arrow through my heart.

I made him sick.

I would never forget his reaction to learning who I was. The memory haunted me.

I still missed him. It was like all the joy had been sucked out of my life in his absence.

"For years you complained about our German rivals," I said. "Now I am dealing with them and you want me to stop. Make up your mind, Ilya."

"When was the last time you slept?"

It was pointless to answer. We both knew I wasn't sleeping. My mind was a fog of exhaustion, a headache my constant companion.

"Nikolai," he said softly. "Look at me."

Taking a deep breath, I met my friend's gaze. He said, "We have known one another a long time. You are like a brother to me. I would gladly take a bullet for you. But I cannot stand by and watch you destroy yourself."

"I am fine. You are worrying for nothing."

"You miss him."

"Do *not* speak to me of him," I snarled. "This was expected. And it could never be anything else, so drop it."

Ilya's dark eyes studied my face intently. "If you could get out, would you?"

He was trying my patience. "I am not in the mood for games. Continue at your own peril, *mudak*."

"It is a serious question. If you could leave the brotherhood, would you?"

"You speak in riddles. There is no leaving, as we both know. The brotherhood is our life until we die."

Ilya stared at the clock on the wall, then he checked his mobile. "That is what I thought you might say. I hope you will forgive me."

"Forgive you for what?"

It happened in a blink.

A deafening sound, then the building shook all around us. There was no chance to seek cover, to prepare myself, before I was thrown to the ground. Something landed on top of me. The desk?

Then everything went black.

CHAPTER TWELVE

Theo

"Did you sleep here again?" Sofia, my assistant, set a demitasse of caffè on my desk. The lines of her forehead were creased in concern as she studied my rumpled appearance. "I could swear those are the clothes you wore yesterday."

Ignoring the question, I frowned at the calendar on my laptop screen. "Why is there a fitting on my schedule? I've never heard of this person, and you know I don't do fittings for random customers anymore."

"He insisted. And he slipped me five thousand Euros to put him on your calendar."

I lifted a brow at her. "Taking bribes? That seems unethical of you."

She shrugged. "He also paid your fee in advance, in addition to the twenty-five suits he's ordered. You're welcome."

"*Ma dai*. I should fire you," I grumbled as I opened the appointment notes. The man's name was Mr. Schmidt, a banker from Munich. No photo.

"But you won't, because you love me. And I am the best assistant you've ever had."

Unfortunately, this was true. "Has security signed off on this?"

"Yes, of course."

Relieved, I sipped my caffè. One couldn't be too careful after falling in love with—and then leaving—a Russian monster.

No one at work knew what happened on my vacation because I was excellent at hiding a broken heart. Except for sleeping in my office, I was holding it together. I kept up with my responsibilities and always smiled. Best of all, my new designs for next season were absolute fire, the collection coming together perfectly.

If you are afraid of wolves, you won't go into the forest.

I wasn't afraid any longer—I'd already gone into the forest and escaped the wolf. So fuck the critics. They couldn't hurt me, not in any lasting way because Nikolai had taken care of that. There was nothing left for anyone else to take.

I was empty inside.

But I was alive—and I planned to stay that way. Upon returning to Paris, I changed my number and hired a top-level security firm. Now there were cameras around my office and home. I looked over my shoulder in public, and declined invitations to all events. I rarely went home, where I had too much time to think.

It was bad enough that Nikolai haunted my dreams. I didn't need him ruining my days, as well.

Work kept me busy for the next few hours. There were calls with manufacturers, meetings with production designers and my design team. Paris Fashion Week was only two weeks away, but we were ahead of schedule due to my relentless pace.

"Your fitting is here," Sofia said as I looked over some fabric samples. "I put him in the small studio upstairs."

"This is the last one, Sofia," I said, sighing. "No matter what they pay you."

She held up her hands. "Understood. He's very handsome, if that helps."

No, it did not. I was not interested in men at the moment. "You are coming with me to take notes."

Once she grabbed her tablet, we headed up to the small studio. I pushed through the door first, then stopped in my tracks.

Nikolai.

Oh, my god. Nikolai was here, in my studio. Tall and broad, with his familiar dark features bathed in warm sunlight. His jaw was sharper, his cheekbones more pronounced. Has he lost weight?

Then I noticed the scratches on his face. Has he been hurt? Bratva business gone bad?

Turning, I blocked the door so Sofia couldn't enter. "You may go. I have this handled."

She cocked her head, but didn't argue. "See you downstairs."

When she was gone I took a deep breath and pulled myself together. *Don't let on that you know.* "Nikolai."

"Hello, *solnyshko.*"

Dio mio, that deep rough voice. It sank under my skin and down into my bones. I fought to keep a straight face. "This is a surprise."

"I had to see you."

"Why?"

His big frame rose and fell on a heavy sigh. "To apologize."

"For?"

"You don't need to pretend. I know you know."

My heart began thumping, racing, like the organ was trying to force its way out of my chest. Was this it? Was he here to silence me, to ensure his secret never got out?

Still, I played dumb. "I have no idea what you're talking about."

He slipped his hands into his trouser pockets. "There are video cameras all over the yacht."

Merda. Why hadn't I realized this? He obviously saw me eavesdropping outside his office door. What was he going to do now? My stomach clenched.

If he was here to kill me, I would not make it easy on him.

"Do not stare at me like that," he said quietly.

"Like what?"

"Like I might hurt you." When I remained silent, he dragged a hand down his face. "I won't hurt you, Theo. I can't. I'd rather cut off both my hands first."

Despite this vow, I rushed to say, "I won't tell anyone your secret."

"I know."

He did? I thought he was here to intimidate me. To scare me into silence. "Then why are you here?"

"I had to see you. I have been miserable the last five weeks. I . . . ." He grimaced, like this conversation was painful. "I miss you."

"You shouldn't have come. It's too risky for both of us."

"I know I hurt you. I am so sorry, Theo. If there had been any other way—"

"There was another way," I reminded him. "You could have been honest with me."

"Impossible!" He nearly shouted, then tempered his voice. "And you know why. It meant death for me. And if I told you, you never would have agreed to one night in my hotel, let alone two weeks on my yacht."

"So you lied."

"I never lied. I just never told you what I did for a living."

"Which is a lie by omission."

"And you never asked," he continued. "With the guns and the yacht, you had to suspect. Yet you never questioned it."

"So I'm at fault for not casually working murder and human trafficking into a conversation?"

"No." He angled his head and stared at the wall. "And I never sold flesh of any kind."

I was relieved to hear it, but in the end it didn't matter. "You've wasted your time in coming here. We're through."

"No."

My jaw fell open. "You don't get to decide, Nikolai. You are not free to live openly, and I refuse to hide in hotel rooms and on yachts for the rest of my life. I am not going back into the closet ever again."

"I am not asking you to do that."

"Oh? Then what do you propose? I give up my life to join the Bratva? Because that will never happen."

He reached inside his suit coat and withdrew a folded newspaper. He threw it onto the ground at my feet. The headline was in Russian, and there was a grainy photo of an older man on it. "What is this?"

"My obituary." He tilted his chin toward the story. "Nikolai Kuznetsov is dead."

CHAPTER THIRTEEN

Nikolai

I watched the man I love absorb this news. Theo stared hard at the newspaper, as if waiting for the letters to rearrange themselves into something he could read.

Dressed in a pair of slim jeans, boots, and ripped t-shirt, he looked so fucking good. His hair was longer, slicked back off his forehead, and there were deep circles under his eyes. I wondered if they were because of me.

"Is this a joke?" he asked.

"No. Not a joke." A lot of effort and planning had gone into creating a new identity for me after the bombing. The Bratva had to believe me dead for this to work.

But there was no going back. Ilya had done this for me, my brother in everything but blood. After I regained consciousness, he had given me the choice. Declare Nikolai Kuznetsov dead and go live a free life . . . or continue to serve as pakhan and forget ever meeting Theo.

The choice had been easy.

I had a chance at happiness, a life with the most amazing man I'd ever known. I loved him, and it was worth giving up my position, the brotherhood, everything, for a chance at having Theo by my side.

Besides, I had all the money a person needed, stashed in places the Bratva couldn't touch. So why was I resigning myself to a life of misery? Of loneliness? I'd found the man I wanted above all others and experienced a slice of the blissful future we could have together.

What was I waiting for?

Quickly, we put a plan into place, using the bombing as cover for my escape. Now I was a wealthy banker from Munich with a slight Russian accent. For the first time I could see a path forward. A way out.

And I wasn't giving up until Theo agreed to join me.

His eyebrows shot up in disbelief. "You left the Bratva?"

"In a manner of speaking. I could not quit, so I used this bombing to fake my death."

"Why?"

"For you. I faked my death for *you*. Ilya helped me."

He didn't say anything. Not a good sign.

Panic rose in my chest and I pressed on. "I miss you. I want to be with you."

"And you think it's this easy? You want this, so I will want it, too?"

"No, of course not."

He bent to pick up the paper and stared at it. "This is unbelievable. I didn't ask you to do this for me. I have my own life here. I can't go on the run with you."

"No one is going on the run," I said calmly. "Ilya has taken over as pakhan. Only he knows I am alive. This will stay a secret."

"I've seen the movies. The mafia, the Bratva do not allow people to leave. You need to go into hiding. Someone will see you."

"I'll grow a beard, if you like. Besides, no one will recognize me. Bratva pakhans are not exactly celebrities. Did you find any information on me when you were searching online?"

"No. But Giulio and Alessio knew you. So you're not a complete mystery."

"Ricci was trailing an associate in Minsk. I made the mistake of taking a rare face-to-face meeting with this associate and the assassin saw me. But there are not many like Alessandro Ricci."

"And you think no one will question this?" He held up the paper.

"No." He didn't appear to believe me, so I continued. "Everyone will believe this was Nikolai Kuznetsov."

"What about the men under your command? They knew what you looked like."

"Ilya is in charge and he will protect me. My men are now loyal to him." When he continued to stare at me, I placed my hand over my heart. "I would not come here and risk your life if I were not one hundred percent sure it was safe for you."

"What about the life you'll be leaving behind?" asked Theo. "How will you give up the power, the money, the—God, I can't believe I'm saying this—the perks of the job?"

"You don't understand. I left my life behind a long time ago when I was a young man and realized I could never be who I really was inside. This is my chance to get my life *back*. You helped me see that. This is a chance for me to be happy. With you."

He didn't appear convinced. "Why didn't you tell me?"

"I was trying to protect us both. I thought we would spend a few weeks fucking, then you would return to Paris."

"Yes, I heard what you said to Giulio." He dropped his voice to do a terrible Russian accent. "'He will return to Paris next week, none the wiser.'"

My skin heated. I hated that he overheard this. "I tried. I thought giving you up was for the best. But I didn't know what it would feel like to be without you, how miserable it would be. I miss you, *solnyshko*."

Theo bit his bottom lip and stared through the windows, his eyes suspiciously glassy. Had I upset him?

I couldn't bear the thought.

Closing the distance between us, I didn't stop until we were nearly toe-to-toe. I stared down at this gorgeous man, my limbs vibrating with the need to feel him, to comfort him. "May I touch you?"

He gave me a small nod, so I stroked the smooth skin of his cheek with one finger. He shivered and that tiny gesture gave me hope. It was a good sign that I still affected him so strongly, yes?

"I don't understand this," he whispered. "We've known one another for a hot minute. So why does it hurt so badly to be without you?"

"Time is irrelevant when you find the person you are meant to spend the rest of your life with. You are that person for me." After all the secrecy, I owed him the truth. I took a deep breath. "I am in love with you."

I got a brief look at his ravaged face before it disappeared into the side of my throat. His arms went around me, but I wasn't sure if this was a good sign. I held him tight, breathing him in, as the panic began to mount. Was this it? Would he tell me to leave him alone? Had I not done enough to get him back?

I wasn't sure what more I could do.

"I can give you more time," I rasped. "I know you aren't ready and I've hurt you. But I won't give up. I will stay in Paris and—"

"Nic, stop. I don't need more time." He shifted to rest his forehead against my cheek. "I think I'm in love with you, too. I've never felt this way about anyone, like we're connected. Like you understand me better than anyone else. I am lost without you, *mon grand*."

Happiness raced through me and I couldn't stand it any longer. Desperate to kiss him, I pressed our mouths together. He rose up on his toes and opened his lips, letting me in, and I took full advantage. My tongue stroked against his, tasting and twining, and I dragged greedy hands over every part of him I could touch, reacquainting myself with the feel of him. Fuck, I had missed this.

He eased back, but still clutched my shoulders. "I don't like secrets."

I held his face in my palms. "There are no more secrets between us, ever. And I am never hiding you again. I am proud to stand at your side."

His mouth hitched as his eyes softened. "And I am proud to have you at my side, Mr. Schmidt of Munich. Though I'm not sure anyone will believe that is really your name."

"I don't give a fuck what they believe. Besides, everyone will be too busy looking at you to focus on me."

"Not if you let me design clothes for you," he said, sweeping his palms over my shoulders. "You're like a giant blank canvas waiting to be brought to life."

I smiled as I bent my head to kiss him again. "No, I'm not. You brought me to life the instant we met, *solnyshko*."

His breath hitched and his fingers tightened on me. "*Mon dieu*, such poetry. I might swoon like one of Brontë's heroines if you keep that up."

"Who is Brontë?"

He gaped up at me, offended. "*Mon grand!* Have you not read the classics like Austen and Brontë? Heathcliff? Darcy?" When I frowned and shook my head, Theo's expression turned devious. "Oh, I have so much to teach you, Mr. Schmidt."

I kissed his mouth hard. "And I look forward to every minute of it."

EPILOGUE

Theo

June, Almost One Year Later
Paris Fashion Week

It was great.

I knew it was great. The best collection I'd ever designed.

Even still, when I came out at the end of the show, I hadn't expected everyone to be on their feet, cheering.

A lump settled in my throat. The approval, a validation of all my hard work, was something I never took for granted.

But there was one person's approval that meant more to me than anything else in the world. I searched him out immediately, the love of my life.

Nic.

He went by Nicholas Schmidt now, with a heavy beard to cover his face, but I would know those bright blue eyes anywhere. I found him on his feet, applauding loudly. I smiled and put my hand over my heart.

He did the same.

Phones were aimed at us from all around the room, but I didn't care. *Cazzo*, I loved this man.

The models surrounded me, clapping along with everyone else. I bowed and waved to the crowd. Then we filed off the stage and went behind the curtain. I hugged and kissed each of the models, along with my staff, as we celebrated. This collection had been a true labor of love.

Bello e Brutto.

The pieces were bold and ugly, yet elegant, and blurred the lines of the antiquated ideas of gender identity into something new. In the past I designed for men, but this was a collection that could be worn by anyone.

"This was fantastic. Your best yet!" one of the makeup artists said as she kissed my cheek. "Bravo, Signore Barella!"

"*Grazie, grazie.*"

A glass of champagne was thrust into my hand. We toasted and celebrated, then the models and staff began to disperse as the celebrities and fashion industry elites arrived. I chatted with the star of an award-winning film, then a newspaper editor next. A blogger, a famous chef. It went on and on, and I soaked in the attention.

I was a Leo, after all.

Soon the crowd thinned and I was able to see him, waiting for me on the edge of the room. He never interrupted or barged his way in. He let me be stand in the spotlight and I loved him for it. He was supportive in every way, my wolf who helped me conquer my fears.

And life after the Bratva agreed with my man. Nightmares were rare these days, and he was more relaxed. Happier. Now he was a businessman, a silent partner in a few charities for LGBTQ+ youth and troubled teens. Together, we were starting a foundation to send underprivileged kids to study fashion design for free.

He was everything I'd ever wanted in a partner.

Except he wasn't alone at the moment. Two men were standing with him, and they were all looking at me.

I frowned as I finished my champagne and set the empty flute on a table. I recognized the men, of course. And I didn't know if I was ready to see either of them.

Leo, remember? We didn't like when our loyalty wasn't returned.

As if Nic realized my struggle, he led the men over to me. He kissed me on the mouth, uncaring of who saw. "*Ya tebya lyublyu*. It was fantastic."

I murmured the Russian for *I love you* back to him. He'd been teaching me his native language for the last few months.

Then I faced Giulio and Alessio. They both looked tan from the Spanish sunshine. I knew from Nic that they were now successful mobsters, controlling the crime in Málaga. "This is a surprise," I said stiffly. I didn't move in to kiss cheeks, a harsh insult from an Italian.

Giulio's brow furrowed with unhappiness. "*Amico*. Congratulations." Uncaring of my impoliteness, he gripped my shoulders and kissed both of my cheeks. "I am happy for you, Theo. Truly."

"*Grazie*," I murmured.

Alessio said nothing, but I didn't expect it. In public he was paranoid and vigilant against threats to his *ragazzo*.

Giulio sighed, but didn't release me. "I am sorry. How many times must I apologize before you forgive me?"

"I don't know what you are talking about," I lied. "I'm not angry with you, Don Ravazzani."

"Theo," Nic admonished, his tone making it clear he was disappointed in me. I wasn't surprised. Nic had been trying to mend the broken fences between me and Giulio for awhile now.

"I told you this was a bad idea, Nic," Giulio said, shoving his hands into his trouser pockets. "And I understand how he feels, being lied to by one you trust. It's no less than I deserve."

"This is bullshit." Nic pulled me against his side, his arm around my waist. "We're happy now," he whispered against my temple. "He knew I would never hurt you, that I loved you. Do not continue to punish him, *solnyshko*."

"But—"

"No buts. This ends now. It's been almost a year and you miss him."

"Oh?" Giulio leaned in, the hint of a smile on his face. "Tell me more."

"A little," I clarified, before he could let this go to his head. "I miss you a very little amount." I held up my thumb and forefinger, showing the tiniest sliver of air between them.

"*Cazzata*, as you like to say," Nic added. "Be honest."

"Fine. I do miss our friendship," I told Giulio. "But I'm still hurt and angry."

"I know. Again, I am sorry. I should've warned you, but I could see how you felt about him. And we would've intervened if it hadn't been reciprocated, if you needed help. We've kept tabs on you this whole time."

That was news to me.

"You have?"

Giulio looked to Alessio, who nodded. "I have a friend in Paris," the assassin said quietly. "She reports back to us."

I glanced up at Nic. "Did you know this?"

"Of course." He appeared offended. "I notice everything when it comes to your safety."

"Why didn't you tell me?"

"Because I knew who was responsible and why they were doing it, even though it was unnecessary." His thumb swept soothingly over the small of my back. "It is time to forgive, *luchik*."

"Why?" I was being petulant and I knew it. But I couldn't help it.

Nic's mouth curved into a sly smile. "Because I plan to marry you soon, and you might need a best man."

My lips parted on a shaky breath. This was the first we'd ever discussed marriage. I mean, I knew I never wanted another man, but Nic hadn't said anything about a lifelong commitment before. "Did you say soon?" I wheezed.

"Soon," he declared, his fingers pressing into my flesh to draw me even closer. He pressed his lips to my forehead. "You make me happy, Theo. There is no one else for me."

Could this day get any more perfect?

Chest full of butterflies, I realized Nic was right. I missed Giulio and our friendship. He'd made a mistake and apologized for it. Was I so small and petty that I could not forgive him?

Drawing in a deep breath, I let it out slowly. "I forgive you," I told Giulio.

"Thank fuck!" my friend exclaimed before pulling me in for a hug. I patted his back a few times, but Giulio showed no signs of letting me go. "*Ti voglio bene*," he whispered, an endearment between family and friends.

"*Ti voglio bene*," I repeated and he finally released me. Alessio and Nic both appeared relieved.

I gave Giulio my sweetest smile. "Do you know how you can make this up to me?"

Little lines bracketed Giulio's mouth as worry crept into his expression. "I'm almost afraid to ask, but how?"

"I have a wedding to plan and the Ravazzani estate in Siderno would be the perfect location."

Giulio's jaw fell open, while Alessio sounded as if he was choking on air. When he recovered, Giulio started laughing. "I will ask my father if he minds. If he agrees, then of course. But Spain is nice too, *amico*. We have a large home right on the water."

"How large?" I asked.

"Come visit and see for yourself."

Hand on Nic's stomach, I leaned back to see his face. "Are you ready for a holiday, *mon grand?*"

He kissed my forehead, his lips warm and soft. "I go wherever you go. Always."

ACKNOWLEDGMENTS

Thank you for reading MAFIA DEVIL! This series has literally changed my life, so I'm truly grateful for each and every one of you!

And hey, I'd love an honest review after you're finished, if you feel so inclined.

Remember, join my newsletter for bonus content, book news, links to merch, and more!

Many hands help make these books shine. Thank you to Peter Senftleben for his editing and to Letitia at RBA Designs for the sexy covers. Diana Quincy deserves so much credit, because she always reads my books first and helps me sort out the mess.

So many people help with the chaos of my author life that I'd never be able to properly thank all of them here. But Nicole is the queen who keeps things running smoothly, allowing me to focus on writing. I'm very thankful for all she does!

I would be nothing without my very own Paparino, who helps me with these books and dinner and laundry and a thousand other things that make it possible for me to write. Ti amo, baby.

More books coming soon!

xox,

Mila

Mila Finelli is the dark contemporary pen name of *USA Today* bestselling historical author Joanna Shupe, who finally decided to write the filthy mafia kings she's been dreaming about for years. She's addicted to coffee, travel, and books with bad men.

For signed books, merch, news & more, visit Mila's website at milafinelli.com.

Join Mila's Famiglia on Facebook!

Want more Fausto?
Sign up for Mila's newsletter and get a FREE Fausto &
Frankie bonus story!

ALSO BY MILA FINELLI

THE KINGS OF ITALY SERIES

MAFIA MISTRESS

MAFIA DARLING

MAFIA MADMAN

MAFIA TARGET

MAFIA DEVIL

MAFIA VIRGIN

———

Start at the beginning with Mafia Mistress

Book 1 in the Kings of Italy series!

MAFIA MISTRESS

FAUSTO

I am the darkness, the man whose illicit empire stretches around the globe.

Not many have the courage for what needs to be done to maintain power . . . but I do.

And I always get what I want.

Including my son's fiancée.

She's mine now, and I'll use Francesca any way I see fit. She's the perfect match to my twisted desires, and I'll keep her close, ready and waiting at my disposal.

Even if she fights me at every turn.

FRANCESCA

I was stolen away and held prisoner in Italy, a bride for a mafia king's only heir.

Except I'm no innocent, and it's the king himself—the man called il Diavolo—who appeals to me in sinful ways I never dreamed. Fausto's wickedness draws me in, his power like a drug. And when the devil decides he wants me, I'm helpless to resist him—even if it means giving myself to him, body and soul.

He may think he can control me, but this king is about to find out who's really the boss.

MAFIA MISTRESS is available in eBook, Print and Audio.

www.ingramcontent.com/pod-product-compliance
Lightning Source LLC
Chambersburg PA
CBHW060506300726
48975CB00008B/2663